Edward Ellis

Through Forest and Fire

Edward Ellis

Through Forest and Fire

1st Edition | ISBN: 978-3-73406-015-1

Place of Publication: Frankfurt am Main, Germany

Year of Publication: 2019

Outlook Verlag GmbH, Germany.

Reproduction of the original.

WILD-WOODS SERIES—No. 1.

THROUGH FOREST AND FIRE

BY

EDWARD S. ELLIS,

AUTHOR OF "YOUNG PIONEER SERIES," "LOG CABIN SERIES," "DEERFOOT SERIES," "WYOMING SERIES," ETC., ETC.

PHILADELPHIA:
PORTER & COATES.

"Heavenly Father! please take care of me," prayed Nellie.

PORTER & COATES.

CONTENTS.

THROUGH FOREST AND FIRE;

OR,

"God Helps Them that Help Themselves."

CHAPTER I.

NICK.

Nicholas Ribsam was a comical fellow from his earliest babyhood, and had an original way of doing almost everything he undertook.

When he became big enough to sit on the porch of the humble little home, where he was born, and stare with his great round eyes at the world as it went by, that world, whether on horseback, in carriage, or on foot, was sure to smile at the funny-looking baby.

Nick, although born in western Pennsylvania, was as thoroughly Dutch as if he had first opened his eyes on the banks of the Zuyder Zee, in the lowlands of Holland. His parents had come from that part of the world which has produced so many fine scholars and done so much for science and literature. They talked the language of the Fatherland, although they occasionally ventured on very broken English for the instruction of the boy and girl which heaven had given them.

When Nick was a year old, he seemed as broad as he was long, and his round, red cheeks, big, honest eyes, and scanty hair, which stood out in every direction, always brought a smile to whomsoever looked at him.

"That's the Dutchest baby I ever saw!" exclaimed a young man, who, as he threw back his head and laughed, expressed the opinion of about every one that stopped to admire the youngster.

When we add that Nick was remarkably good natured, his popularity will be understood. Days and weeks passed without so much as a whimper being heard from him. If his mother forgot she was the owner of such a prize, and allowed him to remain on the porch until he was chilled through or half famished, she was pretty sure to find him smiling, when she suddenly

7

awakened to her duties respecting the little fellow.

Several times he tipped over and rolled off the porch, bumping his head against the stones. A hoarse cry instantly made known the calamity but by the time he was snatched up (often head downward) his face was illumined again by his enormous grin, even though the big teardrops stood on his cheeks.

When he grew so as to be able to stand with the help of something which he could grasp, a board about a foot and a half high was placed across the lower part of the open door to prevent him getting outside.

The first day fat little Nick was confronted with this obstruction he fell over it, out upon the porch. How he managed to do such a wonderful thing puzzled father and mother, who half believed some person or animal must have "boosted" him over; but, as there was no other person in sight and they did not own a dog, the explanation was not satisfactory.

True, they had a big Maltese cat, but he was hardly strong enough, even if he had the disposition, to hoist a plump baby over such a gate, out of pure mischief.

But the most remarkable thing took place the next week, when Nick not only fell out of the door and over the obstruction, but a few minutes later fell in again. In fact, it looked as if from that time forward Nick Ribsam's position was inverted almost as often as it was upright.

"There's one thing I want my little boy to learn," said the father, as he took him on his knee and talked in the language of his Fatherland "and that is, 'God helps them that help themselves.' Don't ever forget it!"

"Yaw, I ish not forgots him," replied the youngster, staring in the broad face of his parent, and essaying to make use of the little English he had picked up.

The good father and mother acted on this principle from the beginning. When Nick lost his balance he was left to help himself up again; when he went bumping all the way down the front steps, halting a moment on each one, his father complacently smoked his long pipe and waited to see how the boy was going to get back, while the mother did not think it worth while to leave her household duties to look at the misfortunes of the lad.

"God helps them that help themselves."

There is a great deal in this expression, and the father of Master Nicholas Ribsam seemed to take in the whole far-reaching truth. "You must do everything you possibly can," he said, many a time; "you must use your teeth, your hands, and your feet to hang on; you must never let go; you must hammer away; you must always keep your powder dry; you must fight to the last breath, and all the time ask God to help you pull through, and *He'll do it!*"

This was the creed of Gustav Ribsam and his wife, and it was the creed which the children drew in with their breath, as may be said; it was such a grand faith that caused Nick to develop into a sturdy, self-reliant, brave lad, who expected to take his own part in the battle of life without asking odds from any one.

The parents of our hero and heroine proved their faith by their works. By hard, honest toil and economy, they had laid up a competence which was regularly invested each year, and of which the children were not allowed to know anything, lest it might make them lazy and unambitious.

The little house and fifty acres were paid for, and the property was more than sufficient to meet the wants of the family, even after the youngsters became large enough to go to school.

The morning on which young Nick Ribsam started for the country school, a half mile away, was one which he can never forget. He was six years old, and had picked up enough of the English language to make himself understood, though his accent was of that nature that it was sure to excite ridicule on the part of the thoughtless.

As Nick had a large head, he wore of necessity a large cap, with a long frontispiece and with a button on the top. His coat was what is called a "roundabout," scarcely reaching to his waist, but it abounded with pockets, as did the vest which it partly inclosed. His trousers were coarse, thick, and comfortable, and his large boots were never touched by blacking, Nick's father having no belief in such nonsense, but sticking to tallow all the time.

Nick carried a spelling book and slate under his arm, and, as he started off, any one looking at him would have been struck by his bright eyes, ruddy cheeks, and generally clean appearance. As he was so very good natured, he was certain to become quite an acquisition to the school.

There are no more cruel, or perhaps thoughtless people in the world than a number of school-boys, under certain conditions. The peculiar dress and the broken language of little Nick excited laughter at once, and this soon turned into ridicule.

Nick was beset continually at recess and at noon by the boys, who immediately christened him "Dutchy." He laughed and did not seem to mind it, for his philosophy was that no words applied to him could injure him, and so long as the boys kept their hands off he did not care.

Among the pupils was Herbert Watrous, a spruce young gentleman from the city, who dressed better than the others, and who threw out hints about the sparring lessons he had taken at home, and his wish that he might soon have a chance to show his playmates how easily he could vanquish an opponent, much larger than himself, by reason of his "science."

He was fully four years older than Nick, and much taller—a fact which Herbert regretted as the Pennsylvania Hollander was too insignificant for him to pick a quarrel with.

But that was no reason, as he looked at his privileges in this life, why he should not play the tyrant and bully over the honest little fellow and he proceeded at once to make life unbearable to Nicholas.

He began the cry of "Dutchy," and, finding that it did not disturb the serenity of the lad, he resorted to more active measures on the way home from school.

He began by knocking off his hat, and when Nick looked at him in a surprised way and asked why he did it, the city youth assumed a pugilistic attitude and answered, "Greens; what are you going to do about it, Dutchy?"

"Be careful of him," whispered one of the boys, who felt some sympathy for Nick in his persecutions; "he's *science.*"

"I don't care vat he ain't," replied Nick, beginning to lose his temper; "if he don't lets me be, he'll got into trouble."

Just then Nick started to overtake a lad, who tapped him on the back and invited him to play a game of tag. As he passed close to Herbert, that boy threw out his foot and Nick went sprawling headlong, his book and slate flying from under his arm, while his cap shot a dozen-feet in another direction.

The other boys broke into laughter, while several of the girls cried out that it was a shame.

Nick picked himself up, and putting on his cap, turned about to ask Herbert what he meant by such cruelty, when he was confronted by the bully, who had thrown himself into his fancy pugilistic posture, and with one eye shut and his tongue thrust out, said:

"What are you going to do about it, Dutchy?"

"I'll show you vot I do!"

CHAPTER II.

SCHOOL DAYS.

Nicholas Ribsam proceeded to show Master Herbert Watrous what he meant to do about it.

Paying no heed to the formidable attitude of the city youth, Nick rushed straight upon him, and embracing him about the waist so as to pinion his arms, he threw him flat upon the ground with great emphasis. Then, while Herbert lay on his face, vainly struggling to rise, Nick sat down heavily on his back. Although he could have used his fists with great effect, Nick declined to do so; but, rising some six or eight inches, he sat down on him again, and then repeated the performance very fast, bounding up and down as a man is sometimes seen to do when a horse is trotting; descending each time on the back of Herbert with such vigor that the breath was almost forced from his body.

"Let me up!" shouted the victim, in a jerky, spasmodic manner, as the words were helped out; "that ain't the right way to fight: that isn't fair."

"It suits me better as nefer vas," replied the grinning Nick, banging himself down on the back of the struggling Herbert, until the latter began to cry and ask the boys to pull Nick off.

No one interfered, however, and when the conqueror thought he had flattened out the city youth to that extent that he would never acquire any plumpness again, he rose from his seat and allowed Herbert to climb upon his feet.

Never was a boy more completely cowed than was this vaunting youth, on whom all the others had looked with such admiration and awe. He meekly picked up his hat, brushed off the dirt, and looking reproachfully at Nick said:

"Do you know you broke two of my ribs?"

"I dinks I brokes dem *all*: dat's what I meant to do; I will try him agin."

"No, you won't!" exclaimed Herbert, darting off in a run too rapid for the short legs of Nick to equal.

Nick Ribsam had conquered a peace, and from that time forth he suffered no persecution at school. Master Herbert soon after went back to his city home, wondering how it was that a small, dumpy lad, four years younger than he, was able to vanquish him so completely when all the science was on the side of the elder youth.

Young as was Nick Ribsam, there was not a boy in the school who dared attempt to play the bully over him. The display he had given of his prowess won the respect of all.

Besides this he proved to be an unusually bright scholar. He dropped his faulty accent with astonishing rapidity, and gained knowledge with great facility. His teacher liked him, as did all the boys and girls, and when he was occasionally absent he was missed more than half a dozen other lads would have been.

The next year Nick brought his sister Nellie to school. He came down the road, holding her fat little hand in his, while her bright eyes peered out from under her plain but odd-looking hat in a timid way, which showed at the same time how great her confidence was in her big brother.

Nellie looked as much like Nick as a sister can look like a brother. There were the same ruddy cheeks, bright eyes, sturdy health, and cleanly appearance. Her gingham pantalettes came a little nearer the tops of her shoes, perhaps than was necessary, but the dress, with the waist directly under the arms, would have been considered in the height of fashion in late years.

One daring lad ventured to laugh at Nellie, and ask her whether she had on her father's or mother's shoes, but when Nick heard of it he told the boy that he would "sit down" on any one that said anything wrong to Nellie. Nothing of the kind was ever hinted to the girl again. No one wished to be "sat down" on by the Pennsylvania Hollander who banged the breath so utterly from the body of the city youth who had aroused his wrath.

The common sense, sturdy frame, sound health, and mental strength of the parents were inherited in as marked a degree by the daughter Nellie as by Nick. She showed a quickness of perception greater than that of her brother; but, as is generally the case, the boy was more profound and far-reaching in his thoughts.

After Nick had done his chores in the evening and Nellie was through helping her mother, Gustav, the father, was accustomed to light his long-handled pipe, and, as he slowly puffed it while sitting in his chair by the hearth, he looked across to his boy, who sat with his slate and pencil in hand, preparing for the morrow. Carefully watching the studious lad for a few minutes, he generally asked a series of questions:

"Nicholas, did you knowed your lessons to-day?"

"Yes, sir."

"Did you know efery one dot you knowed?"

"Yes, sir,—every one," answered Nick respectfully, with a quiet smile over his father's odd questions and sentences. The old gentleman could never correct or improve his accent, while Nick, at the age of ten, spoke so accurately that his looks were all that showed he was the child of German parents.

"Did nopody gif you helps on der lessons?"

"Nobody at all."

"Dot is right; did you help anypodies?"

"Yes, sir,—three or four of the girls and some of the boys asked me to give them a lift—"

"Gif dem *vat?*"

"A lift—that is, I helped them."

"Dot ish all right, but don't let me hears dot nopody vos efer helping *you*; if I does—"

And taking his pipe from his mouth, Mr. Ribsam shook his head in a way which threatened dreadful things.

Then the old gentleman would continue smoking a while longer, and more than likely, just as Nick was in the midst of some intricate problem, he would suddenly pronounce his name. The boy would look up instantly, all attention.

"Hef you been into any fights mit nopodies to-day?"

"I have not, sir; I have not had any trouble like that for a long while."

"Dot is right—dot is right; but, Nick, if you does get into such bad tings as fightin', don't ax nopodies to help you; *takes care mit yorself!*"

The lad modestly answered that he did not remember when he had failed to take care of himself under such circumstances, and the father resumed his pipe and brown study.

The honest German may not have been right in every point of his creed, but in the main he was correct, his purpose being to implant in his children a sturdy self-reliance. They could not hope to get along at all times without leaning upon others, but that boy who never forgets that God has given him a mind, a body, certain faculties and infinite powers, with the intention that he should cultivate and use them to the highest point, is the one who is sure to win in the great battle of life.

Then, too, every person is liable to be overtaken by some great emergency which calls out all the capacities of his nature, and it is then that false teaching and training prove fatal, while he who has learned to develop the divine capacities within him comes off more than conqueror.

CHAPTER III.

A MATHEMATICAL DISCUSSION.

The elder Ribsam took several puffs from his pipe, his eyes fixed dreamily on the fire, as though in deep meditation. His wife sat in her chair on the other side, and was busy with her knitting, while perhaps her thoughts were wandering away to that loved Fatherland which she had left so many years before, never to see again. Nellie had grown sleepy and gone to bed.

Mr. Ribsam turned his head and looked at Nick. The boy was seated close to the lamp on the table, and the scratching of his pencil on his slate and his glances at the slip of paper lying on the stand, with the problems written upon it, told plainly enough what occupied his thoughts.

"Nicholas," said the father.

"Just one minute, please," replied the lad, glancing hastily up: "I am on the last of the problems that Mr. Layton gave us for this week, and I have it almost finished."

The protest of the boy was so respectful that the father resumed his smoking and waited until Nick laid his slate on the table and wheeled his chair around.

"There, father, I am through."

"Read owed loud dot sum von you shoost don't do."

"Mr. Layton gave a dozen original problems as he called them, to our class to-day, and we have a week in which to solve them. I like that kind of work, and so I kept at it this evening until I finished them all."

"You vos sure dot you ain't right, Nicholas, eh?"

"I have proved every one of them. Oh, you asked me to read the last one! When Mr. Layton read that we all laughed because it was so simple, but when you come to study it it isn't so simple as you would think. It is this: If New York has fifty per cent. more population than Philadelphia, what per cent. has Philadelphia less than New York?"

Mr. Ribsam's shoulders went up and down, and he shook like a bowl of jelly. He seemed to be overcome by the simplicity of the problem over which his son had been racking his brains.

"Dot makes me laughs. Yaw, yaw, yaw!"

"If you will sit down and figure on it you won't laugh quite so hard," said Nick, amused by the jollity of his father, which brought a smile to his mother;

"what is your answer?"

"If I hafs feefty tollar more don you hafs, how mooch less tollar don't you hafs don I hafs? Yaw, yaw, yaw!"

"*That* is plain enough," said Nick sturdily "but if you mean to say that the answer to the problem I gave you is fifty per cent., you are wrong."

"Oxplains how dot ain't," said Mr. Ribsam, suddenly becoming serious.

The mother was also interested, and looked smilingly toward her bright son. Like every mother, her sympathies went out to him. When Nick told his father that he was in error, the mother felt a thrill of delight; she wanted Nick to get the better of her husband, much as she loved both, and you and I can't blame her.

Nick leaned back in his chair, shoved his hands into his pockets, and looked smilingly at his father and his pipe as he said:

"Suppose, to illustrate, that Philadelphia has just one hundred people. Then, if New York has fifty per cent. more, it must have one hundred and fifty people as its population; that is correct, is it not, father?"

Mr. Ribsam took another puff or two, as if to make sure that his boy was not leading him into a trap, and then he solemnly nodded his head.

"Dot ish so,—dot am,—yaw."

"Then if Philadelphia has one hundred people for its population, New York has one hundred and fifty?"

"Yaw, and Pheelatelphy has feefty per cent. less—yaw, yaw, yaw!"

"Hold on, father,—not so fast. I'm teacher just now, and you mustn't run ahead of me. If you will notice in this problem the per cent. in the first part is based on Philadelphia's population, while in the second part it is based on the population of New York, and since the population of the two cities is different, the per cent. cannot be the same."

"How dot is?" asked Mr. Ribsam, showing eager interest in the reasoning of the boy.

"We have agreed, to begin with, that the population of Philadelphia is one hundred and of New York one hundred and fifty. Now, how many people will have to be subtracted from New York's population to make it the same as Philadelphia?"

"Feefty,—vot I says."

"And fifty is what part of one hundred and fifty,—that is, what part of the population of New York?"

"It vos one thirds."

"And one third of anything is thirty-three and one third per cent. of it, which is the correct answer to the problem."

Mr. Ribsam held his pipe suspended in one hand while he stared with open mouth into the smiling face of his son, as though he did not quite grasp his reasoning.

"Vot you don't laughs at?" he said, turning sharply toward his wife, who had resumed her knitting and was dropping many a stitch because of the mirth, which shook her as vigorously as it stirred her husband a few minutes before.

"I laughs ven some folks dinks dey ain't shmarter don dey vosn't all te vile, don't it?"

And stopping her knitting she threw back her head and laughed unrestrainedly. Her husband hastily shoved the stem of his pipe between his lips, sunk lower down in the chair, and smoked so hard that his head soon became almost invisible in the vapor.

By-and-by he roused himself and asked Nick to begin with the first problem and reason out the result he obtained with each one in turn.

Nick did so, and on the last but one his parent tripped him. A few pointed questions showed the boy that he was wrong. Then the hearty "Yaw, yaw, yaw!" of the father rang out, and looking at the solemn visage of his wife, he asked:

"Vy you don't laughs now, eh? Yaw, yaw, yaw!"

The wife meekly answered that she did not see anything to cause mirth, though Nick proved that he did.

Not only that, but the son became satisfied from the quickness with which his father detected his error, and the keen reasoning he gave, that he purposely went wrong on the first problem read to him with the object of testing the youngster.

Finally, he asked him whether such was not the case. Many persons in the place of Mr. Ribsam would have been tempted to fib, because almost every one will admit any charge sooner than that of ignorance; but the Dutchman considered lying one of the meanest vices of which a man can be guilty. Like all of his countrymen, he had received a good school education at home, besides which his mind possessed a natural mathematical bent. He said he caught the answer to the question the minute it was asked him, and, although Mr. Layton may not have seen it before, Mr. Ribsam had met and conquered similar ones when he was a boy.

While he persistently refused to show Nick how to solve some of the intricate problems brought home, yet when the son, after hours of labor, was still all abroad, his father would ask him a question or two so skillfully framed that the bright boy was quick to detect their bearing on the subject over which he was puzzling his brain. The parent's query was like the lantern's flash which shows the ladder for which a man is groping.

The task of the evening being finished, Mr. Ribsam tested his boy with a number of problems that were new to him. Most of them were in the nature of puzzles, with a "catch" hidden somewhere. Nick could not give the right answer in every instance, but he did so in a majority of cases; so often, indeed, that his father did a rare thing,—he complimented his skill and ability.

CHAPTER IV.

LOST.

It was two miles from the home of Mr. Ribsam to the little stone school-house where his children were receiving their education. A short distance from the dwelling a branch road turned off to the left, which, being followed nine miles or so, mostly through woods, brought one to the little country town of Dunbarton.

Between the home of Gustav Ribsam and the school-house were only two dwellings. The first, on the left, belonged to Mr. Marston, whose land adjoined that of the Hollander, while the second was beyond the fork of the roads and was owned by Mr. Kilgore, who lived a long distance back from the highway.

Nick Ribsam, as he grew in years and strength, became more valuable to his father, who found it necessary, now and then, to keep him home from school. This, however, did not happen frequently, for the parents were anxious that their children should receive a good school education, and Nick's readiness enabled him to recover, very quickly, the ground thus lost.

There was not so much need of Nellie, and, when at the age of six she began her attendance, she rarely missed a day. If it was stormy she was bundled up warmly, and, occasionally, she was taken in the carriage when the weather was too severe for walking.

The summer was gone when Nick helped harness the roan mare to the carriage, and, driving down to the forks, let Nellie out, and kept on toward Dunbarton, while the little girl continued ahead in the direction of the school-house.

"I've got to stay there so long," said Nick, in bidding his sister good-by, "that I won't be here much before four o'clock, so I will look out for you and you can look out for me and I'll take you home."

Nellie said she would not forget, and walked cheerfully up the road, singing a school song to herself.

The little girl, when early enough, stopped at the house of Mr. Marston, whose girl Lizzie attended school. This morning, however, when Nick called from the road, he was told that Lizzie had been gone some time, so he drove on without her.

The dwelling of Mr. Kilgore stood so far back that Nellie never could spare the time to walk up the long lane and back again, but she contented herself with peering up the tree-lined avenue in quest of Sallie and Bobby Kilgore.

However, they were also invisible, and so it was that Nellie made the rest of the journey alone.

The distance being so considerable, Nellie and Nick always carried their dinners with them, so that, after their departure in the morning, the parents did not expect to see them again until between four and five in the afternoon.

The roan mare was young and spirited, but not vicious, and the boy had no trouble in controlling her.

When half way through the stretch of woods they crossed a bridge, whose planks rattled so loudly under the wheels and hoofs that the animal showed a disposition to rear and plunge over the narrow railing at the side.

But the boy used his whip so vigorously that he quickly tamed the beast, which was not slow to understand that her master was holding the reins.

When Nick was on such journeys as these, he generally carried his father's watch, so as to "make his connections" better. The timepiece was of great size and thickness, having been made somewhere in England a good many years before. It ticked so loudly that it sounded like a cricket, and would have betrayed any person in an ordinary sized room, when there was no unusual noise. Nick's own handsome watch was too valuable for him to carry.

The former was so heavy that it seemed to Nick, when walking with it, that he went in a one-sided fashion. However, the lad was quite proud of it, and perhaps took it out oftener than was necessary, especially when he saw the eyes of others upon him.

Nick was kept in Dunbarton so long by the many errands he had to perform, that he was fully an hour late in starting. The mare was spirited enough to make up this time, if urged, but there was no need of doing so, and the boy knew his father would prefer him not to push the animal when no urgency existed.

Thus it came about that when Nick re-entered the main highway that afternoon, and looked in the direction of the school-house, he saw nothing of Nellie, nor indeed of any one coming from the school.

"She has gone home long ago," was his conclusion, as he allowed the mare to drop into a brisk trot, which speedily took him to his house.

When Nick had put away the horse and rendered up his account of the errands done, he was surprised to learn that Nellie had not yet appeared.

"I cannot understand what keeps her," said the father, in his native tongue; "she was never so late before."

It was plain from the mother's face and manner that she also was anxious, for she frequently went to the gate, and, shading her eyes, looked long and anxiously down the road, hoping that the figure of the little girl would come to view, with some explanation of the cause for her delay.

But the sun was low in the west, and its slanting rays brought to light the figure of no child hurrying homeward. The single object that was mistaken for the loved one proved to be a man on horseback, who turned off at the forks and vanished.

"Nick, go look for your sister," said his mother, as she came back from one of these visits to the gate; "something has happened."

The boy was glad of the order, for he was on the point of asking permission to hunt for Nellie.

"I'll stay till I find out something," said Nick, as he donned his hat and took a general look over himself to see that he was in shape, "so don't worry about me."

"But you ought not to be gone so long," said the father, whose anxious face showed that he was debating whether he should not join his boy in the search, "for it won't take long to find out where Nellie is."

"I think she has been taken sick and has stopped with some of the neighbors," ventured the mother, "but it is strange they do not send me word."

And it was the very fact that such word was not sent that prevented the husband and son from believing in the theory of the distressed mother.

But Nick did not let the grass grow under his feet. His worriment was as great as that of his parents, and as soon as he was in the road he broke into a trot, which he kept up until beyond sight, both father and mother standing at the gate and watching him until he faded from view in the gathering twilight.

The point where he disappeared was beyond the house of Mr. Marston, so it was safe to conclude he had learned nothing of his sister there, where he was seen to halt.

There is nothing more wearisome than waiting in such suspense as came to the hearts of the father and mother, while they sat watching and listening for the sound of the childish footsteps and voices whose music would have been the sweetest on earth to them.

The supper on the table remained untasted, and the only sounds heard were the solemn ticking of the old clock, the soft rustling of the kettle on the stove, and now and then a long drawn sigh from father or mother, as one strove to utter a comforting word to the other.

All at once the gate was opened and shut hastily. Then a hurried step sounded along the short walk and upon the porch.

"There they are! there they are!" exclaimed the mother, starting to her feet, as did the father.

Almost on the same instant the door was thrown open, and, panting and excited, Nick Ribsam entered.

But he was alone, and the expression of his face showed that he had brought bad news.

CHAPTER V.

THE PARTY OF SEARCH.

When Nick Ribsam set out to find his missing sister Nellie, he made the search as thorough as possible.

The first house at which he stopped was that of Mr. Marston, which, it will be remembered, was only a short distance away from his own home. There, to his disappointment, he learned that their little girl had not been at school that day, and consequently they could tell him nothing.

Without waiting longer than to give a few words of explanation he resumed his trot, and soon after turned into the lane leading to the home of Mr. Kilgore. He found that both Bobby and Sallie had been to school, but they had nothing to tell. When we are more than usually anxious to learn something, it seems that every one whom we meet is stupid beyond endurance. If we are in a strange place and apply for information, the ignorance of nearly every person is exasperating.

Bobby and Sallie remembered seeing Nellie in school during the forenoon and afternoon, but, while the boy insisted that she came along the road with them after dismissal, Sallie was just as positive that the missing girl was not with them.

The party of school children which usually went over the highway was so small in number that it is hard to understand how such a mistake could be made, but the difference between Bobby and Sallie was irreconcilable.

"I *know* she didn't come home with us," said Sallie, stamping her foot to give emphasis to the words.

"And I *know* she did," declared Bobby, equally emphatically, "for me and her played tag."

"Why don't you say she and I played tag?" asked Nick, impatient with both the children.

"'Cause it was me and her," insisted Bobby.

"What a dunce-head!" exclaimed his sister; "that was *last* night when you played tag, and you tumbled over into the ditch and bellered like the big baby you are."

"I remember that he did that last night," said Nick, hoping to help the two to settle the dispute.

"I know I done that last night, but this afternoon I done it too. I fall into the ditch every night and beller; I do it on purpose to fool them that are chasing me."

Nick found he could gain nothing; but he believed the sister was right and the brother wrong, as afterward proved to be the case.

There were no more houses between his own home and the school building, and Nick resumed his dog trot, never halting until he came in front of a little whitewashed cottage just beyond the stone school-house.

The latter stood at the cross roads, and the cottage to the left was where the teacher, Mr. Layton, an old bachelor, lived with his two maiden sisters.

Mr. Layton, although strict to severity in the school-room, was a kind-hearted man and was fond of the Ribsam children, for they were bright, cheerful, and obedient, and never gave him any trouble, as did some of his other pupils. He listened to Nick's story, and his sympathy was aroused at once.

"I am very sorry," said he, "that your good father and mother, not to mention yourself, should be so sorely troubled; but I hope this is not serious. Nellie came to me about three o'clock and asked whether I would let her go home."

"Was she sick?" asked the distressed brother.

"Not at all; but she said you had gone to Dunbarton in your carriage and she wanted to meet you coming back. She knew her lessons perfectly, and Nellie is such a good girl that I felt that I could not refuse so simple a request. So I told her she could go. I saw her start homeward with her lunch-basket in one hand and her two school-books in the other. She stepped off so briskly and was in such cheerful spirits that I stood at the window and watched her until she passed around the bend in the road."

Nick felt his heart sink within him, for the words of the teacher had let in a great deal of alarming truth upon him.

Nellie had reached the forks two hours ahead of him, and then, not wishing to sit down and wait, she had started up the road in the direction of Dunbarton to meet him. She must have entered the eight mile stretch of woods from the south about the same time Nick himself drove into it on his return from Dunbarton.

The two should have met near Shark Creek, but neither had seen the other. Nick, as a matter of course, had kept to the road, but what had become of Nellie?

This was the question the lad put to himself, and which caused him to feel so faint that he sank down in a chair unable to speak for a minute or two. Then, when he tried to do so, he had to stop, and was kept busy swallowing the lump that would rise in his throat, until finally the tears suddenly appeared, and, putting his hands to his eyes, he gave way to his grief.

"There, there," said Mr. Layton soothingly, "don't cry, Nick, for it will do no good. Nellie has strayed off in the woods to gather flowers or perhaps wild grapes and has missed her way."

"She—is—lost—poor—Nellie!" said the lad as best he could between his sobs; "we'll never see her again."

"Oh, it isn't as bad as that! I suppose she has grown weary, and, sitting down to rest, has fallen asleep."

If the good teacher meant this to soothe the lad, it had the contrary effect, for the picture of his little sister wandering alone in the woods was one of the most dreadful that could be imagined, and it took all the manhood of his nature to keep from breaking down again.

While the interview was under way, Mr. Layton was busy changing his slippers for his boots, his wrapper for his coat, and his hat was donned just as he spoke the last words.

His sympathy did not expend itself in talk, but the instant he saw what the trouble was he was eager to do all he could to help his suffering friends. He even reproached himself for having given Nellie permission to meet her brother, though no matter what harm may have befallen her, no one could blame her instructor therefor.

"We must hunt for her," said Mr. Layton, when he was ready to go out; "I will tell my sisters they need not be alarmed over my absence, and I guess I will take the lantern with me."

Nick passed out to the front gate, where he waited a minute for the teacher, until he should speak with his friends and get the lantern ready. When he came forth, the boy felt much like the patient who sees the surgeon take out his instruments and try their edge to make sure they are in condition before using upon him.

The sight of the lantern in the hand of Mr. Layton gave such emphasis to the danger that it caused another quick throb of Nick's heart, but he forced it down as the two started back over the road, toward the school-house.

"There is no need of lighting the lantern until we get to the woods," said the teacher, "for we don't need it, and I hope we won't need it after we reach the forest. Poor Nellie! she will feel dreadfully frightened, when she wakes up in the dark forest."

He regretted the words, for the two or three sobs that escaped the brother, before he could master himself, showed that his heart was swelled nigh to bursting.

The night was mild and pleasant, although a little too chilly for any one to sleep out of doors. The moon was gibbous, and only a few white, feathery clouds now and then drifted across its face. Where there was no shadow, one could see for a hundred yards or so with considerable distinctness—that is, enough to recognize the figure of a man in motion.

Opposite the lane leading to the house of Mr. Kilgore, the teacher stopped.

"I will go in and get him to join us," said Mr. Layton; "and you had better hurry home for your father. On your way back, stop for Mr. Marston; that will give us a pretty large party. If when you reach the forks you do not find us there, don't wait, but hurry on toward Dunbarton; you will meet us before you reach the bridge over Shark Creek."

Nick did as told, and, still on a rapid trot, reached home panting and excited, with the story which the reader has just learned.

Mr. Ribsam threw down his pipe, donned his hat and coat, and started out the door. With his hand on the latch, he paused, and, looking back, commanded his voice so as to say:

"Katrina, you and Nick needn't wait up for me."

"Oh, father," pleaded the lad, moving toward him: "would you make me stay at home when Nellie is lost?"

"No, no—I did not think," answered the parent, in a confused way; "I feel so bad I do not know what I do and say. Katrina, don't feel too bad; we will come back as soon as we can."

Again the half distracted father placed his hand on the latch, and he had drawn the door partly open, when his wife, pale and trembling, called out in a voice of touching pathos:

"Gustav, my heart would break should I try to stay here, when no one but God knows where my darling Nellie is; but, wherever she may be, no sorrow or pain or suffering can come to her that her mother will not share, and may our Heavenly Father let her mother take it all upon her own shoulders!"

"Come on, Katrina; come on and bring the lantern with you."

CHAPTER VI.

GROPING IN DARKNESS.

When the parents and brother of Nellie Ribsam reached the forks a few minutes later, they saw nothing of the three parties whom they expected to meet there.

"They have gone on to the woods to look for Nellie," said the father.

"They cannot be far off," suggested Nick, turning to the left.

All were too anxious to lose a minute, and they started after their friends on a rapid walk, Nick taking the lead, and now and then dropping into a loping trot, which he would have increased had he been alone.

A chill seemed to settle over all as they reached the deep shadow of the woods, which was one of the largest tracts of forest in that section of the country.

The road which bisected them was fully eight miles in length, as has already been stated, while the forest was much greater in extent in the other direction.

Being of such large area, there were necessarily many portions which rarely if ever were visited by hunters. Years before an occasional deer had been shot, and a few of the old settlers told of the thrilling bear hunts they had enjoyed when they were not so very much younger than now.

Those who were capable of judging were certain that if the gloomy depths were explored these dreaded animals would be met; but if such were the fact, the beasts were so few in number that no one gave them a thought.

It was now four miles to Shark Creek, and, by common consent, it was agreed that the missing Nellie must be found, if found at all, before reaching the stream.

As this creek was deep enough to drown any person who could not swim, not to mention the large pond into which it emptied, every one of the searchers felt a vague, awful dread that poor Nellie had fallen into the water.

No one spoke of it, but the thought was there all the same.

Shortly after entering the wood, Nick called attention to two star-like points of light twinkling ahead of them.

"They are the lanterns of Mr. Layton and Kilgore," said Nick, who immediately added, "we forgot to stop and get Mr. Marston."

"That is too bad, but it isn't worth while to go back now," replied his father, hardly slackening his gait.

As the lantern which Mrs. Ribsam had handed to her husband was lighted before leaving home, the men in advance detected it immediately after they were seen themselves, and the halloo of the teacher was answered by Nick.

"Have you found anything of Nellie?" asked the mother, in broken English, as soon as the parties came together.

"It could scarcely be expected," answered the instructor, in a kindly voice; "we have just got here, and have only looked along the road. I have little doubt that she is soundly sleeping somewhere not far off."

While all stood still, the father lifted up his voice, and in clear, penetrating tones called the name of his missing child:

"Nellie!"

The ticking of the big watch in the pocket of Nick was plainly heard as the little company awaited the answering call of the child.

But it came not, and three times more was the name of the missing girl repeated by the father, who broke down completely the last time.

Nick now joined his thumb and finger against the end of his tongue, and emitted a blast like that of a steam whistle. It resounded among the trees, and then followed the same oppressive stillness as before.

It was useless to remain where they were any longer, and, without a word, the five moved on. The three lamps were swung above their heads, and they peered into the gloomy depths on the right and left.

Nick, as might have been expected, kept the advance, and his father allowed him to carry the lantern. As the other lights were behind the lad, the latter saw his huge shadow continually dancing in front and taking all manner of grotesque shapes, while, if the others had looked to the rear, they would have seen the same spectacle, as it affected their own figures.

"Wait!" suddenly called out the father, who was now obliged to use his broken English, "mebbe my Nellie she does hears me."

Thereupon he called to her as before, Nick ending the appeal with an earsplitting whistle, which must have been heard several miles on such a still night.

Not the slightest result followed, and with heavy hearts the little company moved on again.

"I think," said Mr. Layton, "that she has turned aside, where, possibly, some faint path has caught her eye, and it may be that we may discover the spot."

"Let's look here!"

It was the mother who spoke this time, and, as they turned toward her, she was seen bending over the ground at the side of the highway, where something had arrested her attention.

Instantly all the lanterns were clustered about the spot, and it was seen that the eyes of affection had detected just such a place as that named by the teacher. Persons who walked along the road were accustomed to turn aside into the woods, and the five now did the same, moving slowly, with the lanterns held close to the earth, and then swung aloft, while all eyes were peering into the portions penetrated by the yellow rays.

The path was followed some fifty yards, when, to the disappointment of all, it came back to the road: it was one of those whimsical footways often met in the country, the person who started it having left the highway without any real reason for doing so.

Again the name of the missing Nellie was repeated, and again the woods sent back nothing but the echo.

"Hark!"

It was the quick-eared Nick who spoke, just as the hum of conversation began, and all listened.

As they did so the rattle of wheels was heard coming from the direction of Dunbarton. The peculiar noise enabled the friends to recognize it as made by a heavy, lumbering farmer's wagon. The team was proceeding on a walk.

A few minutes later some one shouted:

"Halloo, there! what's the matter?"

The voice was recognized as that of Mr. Marston, whom they intended to ask to join them.

Instantly a hope was aroused that he might be able to tell them something of Nellie. Mr. Layton called back, saying they were friends, and asking whether the farmer had seen anything of Nellie Ribsam.

At this Mr. Marston whipped up his horses, which were showing some fear of the twinkling lanterns, and halted when opposite to the party of searchers.

"My gracious! is she lost?" asked the good man, forgetting the anguish of his friends in his own curiosity.

"Yes, she started up this road this afternoon toward Dunbarton to meet her brother, who was returning, but, somehow or other, missed him, and we are all anxious about her."

"My gracious alive! I should think you would be: it would drive my wife and me crazy if our Lizzie should be lost in the woods."

"I suppose, from the way you talk," continued the teacher, "that you have seen nothing of her?"

"No, I wish I had, for I tell you these woods are a bad place for a little girl to get lost in. Last March, when we had an inch of snow on the ground, I seen tracks that I knowed was made by a bear, and a mighty big one, too, and—"

But just then a half-smothered moan from the mother warned the thoughtless neighbor that he was giving anything but comfort to the afflicted parents.

"I beg pardon," he hastened to say, in an awkward attempt to apologize; "come to think, I am sure that it wasn't a bear, but some big dog; you know a large dog makes tracks which can be mistook very easy for those of a bear. I'll hurry on home and put up my team and git the lantern and come back and help you."

And Mr. Marston, who meant well, whipped up his horses, and his wagon rattled down the road as he hastened homeward.

CHAPTER VII.

AN ALARMING DISCOVERY.

By this time the searching party began to realize the difficulties in the path of their success.

If, as was believed, or rather hoped, Nellie had fallen asleep in the woods, they were liable to pass within a dozen feet of where she lay without discovering the fact. Should they call to her, or should Nick emit his resounding signal whistle, she might be awakened, provided only such a brief space separated them, but the chances were scarcely one in a thousand that they would be so fortunate.

This view, at the worst, was a favorable one, and behind it rose the phantoms that caused all to shudder with a dread which they dared not utter.

Only a short distance farther they came upon another path which diverged from the side of the road, returning a little ways beyond. There, an unusually careful search was made, and Nick almost split his cheeks in his efforts to send his penetrating whistle throughout the surrounding country. The three men also called out the name of Nellie in their loudest tones, but nothing except the hollow echoes came back to them.

Nick examined the face of his father's watch by the light of the lantern he carried, and saw that it lacked but a few minutes of nine. They had been searching for the lost child, as this proved, for nearly two hours.

"It seems to me," said Mr. Layton, as the party came to a halt, "that we are not likely to accomplish anything by hunting in this aimless fashion."

"What better can we do?" asked Mr. Kilgore.

"Thus far we have been forced to confine ourselves to the road, excepting when we diverge a few feet: this renders our work about the same as if done by a single person. What I propose, therefore, is that we separate."

"How will that help us?"

"It may not, but we shall cover three or four times the amount of space (I judge Mrs. Ribsam would prefer to remain with her husband and son on account of the single lantern), and it follows that some one of us must pass closer to the spot where Nellie is lying."

This seemed a sensible suggestion, and the two men turned to the afflicted father to learn what he thought of it.

He shook his head.

"Not yet,—not yet; we goes a leetle furder."

Nothing was added by way of explanation, and yet even little Nick knew why he had protested: he wished that all might keep together until they reached the creek. If nothing was learned of his child there, then he would follow the plan of the teacher.

But something seemed to whisper to the parent that the place where they would gain tidings of little Nellie was near that dark, flowing water, which, like such streams, seemed to be always reaching out for some one to strangle in its depths.

"Perhaps Mr. Ribsam is right," said the teacher, after a silence which was oppressive even though brief; "we will keep each other's company, for it is lonely work tramping through the woods, where there is no beaten path to follow."

Thereupon the strange procession resumed its march toward the distant town of Dunbarton, pausing at short intervals to call and signal to the missing one.

It was a vast relief to all that the weather continued so mild and pleasant. In the earlier part of the day there were some signs of an approaching storm, but the signs had vanished and the night was one of the most pleasant seen in September.

Had the rain begun to fall, or had the temperature lowered, the mother would have been distracted, for nothing could have lessened the pangs caused by her knowledge that her darling one was suffering. The true mother lives for her children, and their joys and sorrows are hers.

Whenever the wind rustled among the branches around them she shuddered and instinctively drew her own shawl closer about her shoulder; she would have given a year's toil could she have wrapped the thick woolen garment about the tiny form of her loved one, who never seemed so dear to her as

29

then.

"Gustav," she whispered, twitching his elbow, "I want to speak one word to you."

"Speak out; they cannot understand us," he answered, alluding to the fact that they were using their own language.

"Yes, but I don't want Nick to know what I say."

The husband thereupon fell back beside her, and in a tremulous voice she said:

"Do you remember when Nellie was three years old?"

"Of course I remember further back than that: why do you ask?"

"When she had the fever and was getting well?"

"Yes, I cannot forget it; poor girl, her cheeks were so hot I could almost light a match by them; but, thank God, she got over it."

"You remember, Gustav, how cross she was and how hard it was to please her?"

"But that was because she was sick; when she was well, then she laughed all the time, just like Nick when he don't feel bad."

"But—but," and there was an unmistakable tremor in the voice, "one day when she was cross she asked for a drink of water; Nick was sitting in the room and jumped up and brought it to her, but she was so out of humor she shook her head and would not take it from him; she was determined I should hand it to her. I thought she was unreasonable and I told Nick to set it on the bureau, and I let Nellie know she shouldn't have it unless she took it from him; I meant that I wouldn't hand it to her and thereby humor her impatience. She cried, but she was too stubborn to give in, and I refused to hand her the water. Nick felt so bad he left the room, and I was sorry; but Nellie was getting well, and I was resolved to be firm with her. She was very thirsty, for her fever was a terrible one. I was tired and dropped into a doze. By-and-by I heard Nellie's bare feet pattering on the floor, and softly opening my eyes, without stirring I saw her walk hastily to the bureau, catch hold of the tumbler and she drank every drop of water in it. She was so weak and dizzy that she staggered back and threw herself on the bed like one almost dead. The next day she was worse, and we thought we were going to lose her. You saw how hard I cried, but most of my tears were caused by the remembrance of my cruelty to her the night before."

"But, Katrina, you did right," said the father, who heard the affecting incident for the first time. "It won't do to humor children so much: it will spoil them."

"That may be, but I cannot help thinking of that all the time; it would have done no harm to humor Nellie that time, for she was a good girl."

"You speak truth, but—"

The poor father, who tried so bravely to keep up, broke down and was unable to speak. The story touched him as much as it did the mother.

"Never mind, Katrina—"

At that moment Nick called out:

"Here's the bridge!"

The structure loomed through the gloom as it was dimly lighted by the lanterns, and all walked rapidly forward until they stood upon the rough planking.

Suddenly the mother uttered a cry, and stooping down snatched up something from the ground close to the planks.

The startled friends looked affrightedly toward her, and saw that she held the lunch basket of her little daughter in her hand.

CHAPTER VIII.

STARTLING FOOTPRINTS.

On the very edge of the bridge over Shark Creek, the mother of Nellie Ribsam picked up the lunch basket which her daughter had taken to school that morning. It lay on its side, with the snowy napkin partly out, and within it was a piece of brown bread which the parent had spread with golden butter, and which was partly eaten.

No wonder the afflicted woman uttered a half-suppressed scream when she picked up what seemed a memento of her dead child.

While the lanterns were held in a circle around the basket, which the father took from his wife, Mr. Ribsam lifted the piece of bread in his hand. There were the prints made by the strong white teeth of little Nellie, and there was not a dry eye when all gazed upon the food, which the father softly returned to the basket and reverently covered with the napkin.

No one ventured to speak, but the thoughts of all were the same.

Stepping to the railing at the side of the bridge Mr. Layton held his lantern over, Nick and Mr. Kilgore immediately doing the same. The rays extended right and left and far enough downward to reach the stream, which could be seen, dark and quiet, flowing beneath and away through the woods to the big pond, a quarter of a mile below.

In the oppressive stillness the soft rustling of the water was heard as it eddied about a small root which grew out from the shore, and a tiny fish, which may have been attracted by the yellow rays, leaped a few inches above the surface and fell back with a splash which startled those who were peering over the railing of the structure.

The trees grew close to the water's edge, and as the trunks were dimly revealed they looked as if they were keeping watch over the deep creek that flowed between.

The five were now searching for that which they did not wish to find; they dreaded, with an unspeakable dread, the sight of the white face turned upward, with the abundant hair floating about the dimpled shoulders.

Thank heaven, that sight was spared them; nothing of the kind was seen, and a sigh escaped from each.

"We are all tortured by the thought that Nellie has fallen into the creek and been drowned," said the teacher; "but I cannot see any grounds for such fear."

The yearning looks of the parents and brother caused the teacher to explain more fully.

"No child, unless a very stupid one, would stumble from this bridge, and there could have been no circumstances which in my judgment would have brought such a mishap to Nellie."

This sounded reasonable enough, but:

"De basket,—vot of dot?" asked the father.

"She has dropped that from some cause; but that of itself is a favorable sign, for had she fallen accidentally into the water she would have taken it with her."

This sounded as if true, but it did not remove the fears of any one. Even he who uttered the words could not bring himself fully to believe in their truth, for none knew better than he that the evil one himself seems to conspire with guns and pistols that appear to be unloaded, and with water which is thought to be harmless.

All wanted to place faith in the declaration, and no protest was uttered. As nothing was to be seen or learned where they stood, they crossed the bridge and descended the wooded slope until they reached the edge of the stream, which wound its way through the woods to the big pond.

Every heart was throbbing painfully and no one spoke: there was no need of it, for no comfort could be gained therefrom.

Mr. Layton and Kilgore moved carefully up the creek, while Nick and his parents walked toward the pond, which lay to the left.

The two wished to be apart from the others that they might consult without danger of being overheard by those whose hearts were suffering so much anguish.

"It's very strange," said Mr. Kilgore, "that the basket should be found on the bridge: what do you make of it, Mr. Layton?"

The teacher shook his head.

"It is strange, indeed; had there been no water in the creek you could have set it down as certain that the child had not fallen from it, but, as she could not have done so without drowning, I am inclined to think—"

The instructor hesitated, as if afraid to pronounce the dreadful words.

"You think she is drowned?" said his friend, supplying the answer with his own question.

Mr. Layton nodded his head by way of reply, and, holding the lanterns in front, they began groping their way along the margin of the creek.

By raising the lights above their heads the rays reached the opposite bank, lighting up the water between. This was unusually clear, and they could see the bottom some distance from shore.

Both felt that if the body was floating anywhere they could not fail to see it, though the probabilities were that it was already far below them, and would be first discovered by the parents and brother.

"Halloa!" suddenly exclaimed Mr. Layton, lowering his lantern close to the ground, "I don't like *that*."

By way of explanation, he pointed to the damp soil where no vegetation grew: it was directly in front and close to the water, being that portion which was frequently swept by the creek when above its present level.

Parallel to the stream, for a distance of several rods or so, were a number of imprints in the yielding earth, which the first glance showed were made by some large animal.

"It must have been a dog," ventured the teacher, who had little practical knowledge of the animals of the wood.

Mr. Kilgore shook his head.

"It was a bear; there can be no mistake about it. Mr. Marston was right; it was the track of a similar animal which he saw last March."

"You are not mistaken, Mr. Kilgore?"

The farmer answered impatiently:

"I have hunted bears too often to be mistaken; I can tell their trail among a hundred others, and the one which went along here a little while ago was one of the largest of his kind."

CHAPTER IX.

THE LITTLE WANDERER.

Although Nellie Ribsam was only eight years old at the time she was lost in the big woods, yet the results of the training received from her sensible father and mother showed themselves in a marked degree on that memorable occasion.

She had been taught, as was her brother, that under heaven she must rely upon herself to get forward in the world. Nick was rarely if ever allowed to extend her a helping hand in her lessons, and she was given to understand that whatever was possible for her to do must be done without the aid of any one.

As for sitting down and crying when in trouble, without making any effort to help herself, she knew better than to try that when either her father or mother were likely to find it out.

Her intention, when she left school that afternoon before the session closed, was to keep on in the direction of Dunbarton until she met Nick returning.

She turned off at the forks, and did not lessen her gait until she reached the woods. Her rapid walking caused her to feel quite warm, and the cool shade of the woods was refreshing.

She began wandering aimlessly forward, swinging her hat in her hand, singing snatches of school songs, and feeling just as happy as a little girl can feel who is in bounding health, high spirits, and without an accusing conscience.

It was not the time of year for flowers, and Nellie knew better than to look for any. They had drooped and died long ago; but some of the leaves were turning on the trees, and they gave a peculiar beauty to the autumnal forest.

At intervals she caught sight of the cleanly, symmetrical maple, with some of its leaves turning a fiery red and looking like flecks of flame through the intervening vegetation. At the least rustling of the wind some of the leaves came fluttering downward as lightly as flakes of snow; the little brown squirrel scampered up the shaggy trunks and out upon the limbs, where, perching on his hind legs, he peeped mischievously down at the girl, as if inviting her to play hide-and-seek with him; now and then a rabbit, fat and awkward from his gluttony on the richness around him, jumped softly a few steps, then munched rapidly with his jaws, flapped his long silken ears, looked slyly around with his big, pretty eyes, and, as the girl made a rush toward him, he was off like a shot.

The woods were fragrant with ripening grapes and decaying vegetation, and were putting on a garb whose flaming splendor surpassed the hues of spring.

Indeed, everything conspired to win a boy or girl away from study or work, and to cause the wish on the part of both that they might be a bird or squirrel, with no thought of the responsibilities of life.

Nellie Ribsam forgot for the time everything else except her own enjoyment; but by-and-by the woods took on such tempting looks that she turned off from the highway she had been following, with the intention of taking a stroll, which she meant should not lead her out of sight of the road.

The first view which stopped her was that of a large vine of wild grapes.

Some of them were green, some turning, while others were a dark purple, showing they were fully ripe: the last, as a matter of course, were at the top.

These wild grapes were small and tart, inferior to those which grew in the yard of Nellie at home; but they seemed to be trying to hide in the woods, and they were hard to get, therefore they were more to be desired than the choicest Catawba, Isabella, or Concord.

The main vine, where it started from the ground, was as thick as a man's wrist, and it twisted and wound about an oak sapling as if it were a great African constrictor seeking to strangle the young tree. Other vines branched out from the sides until not only was the particular sapling enfolded and smothered, but the greedy vine reached out and grasped others growing near it.

Nellie felt like the fox who found the grapes more tempting the longer he looked at them.

"I'm going to have some of them," she said, and straightway proceeded to help herself.

She climbed as readily as Nick himself could have done, and never stopped until she was so high that the sapling bent far over with her weight. Then she reached out her chubby hand and plucked a cluster of the wild fruit. They were about the size of buckshot, and when her sound teeth shut down on them, the juice was so sour that she shut both eyes and felt a twinge at the crown of her head as though she had taken a sniff of the spirits of ammonia.

But the grapes were none the less delicious for all that; the fact that there seemed to be something forbidden about them added a flavor that nothing else could give.

Nellie had managed to crush a handful of the vinegar-like globules, when she caught sight of another vine deeper in the woods. It was much larger and climbed fully a dozen yards from the ground, winding in and out among the limbs of a ridgy beech, which seemed to be forever struggling upward to get away from the smothering embrace of the vegetable python.

Five minutes later, Nellie was clambering upward like a monkey, never pausing until the bending tree-top warned her that if she went any higher it would yield to her weight.

Nellie disposed of one bunch and that was enough: she concluded that she was not very hungry for grapes and, without eating or even gathering more, she devoted herself to another kind of enjoyment.

Standing with one foot on a limb and the other on one near it, she grasped a branch above her and began swaying back and forth, with the vim and abandon of a child in a patent swing.

The tree bent far over as she swung outward, then straightened up and inclined the other way as her weight passed over to that side. Any one looking at the picture would have said that a general smash and giving away were certain, in which case the girl was sure to go spinning through the limbs and branches, as though driven forth by the springs within the big gun which fling the young lady outward just as the showman touches off some powder.

But a green sapling is very elastic, and, although the one climbed by Nellie bent back and forth like a bow, it did not give way. Her hair streamed from her head, and there was a thrilling feeling as the wind whistled by her ears, and she seemed to be shooting like a bird through space.

All this was well enough, and it was no more than natural that Nellie should have forgotten several important facts: she was so far from the highway that she could not see any one passing over it; the rush of the wind in her ears shut out sounds that otherwise would have been noticed, and she had gone so far and had lingered so long by the way that it was time to look for Nick on his return from Dunbarton, even though he was later than he expected to be.

It was while she was swinging in this wild fashion that her brother drove by on his way home, without either suspecting how close they were to each other.

Nellie displayed a natural, childish thoughtlessness by keeping up this sport for a half hour longer, when she came down to the ground, simply because she was tired of the amusement.

Although out of sight of the road she managed to find her way back to it without trouble. With her lunch basket in hand, she continued in the direction of Dunbarton, taking several mouthfuls of the bread which had been left over at noon.

In this aimless manner she strolled forward, stopping now and then to look at the squirrel or rabbit or the yellow-hued warbler, the noisy and swift-flying finch, the russet-coated thrush, or dark brown and mottled woodpecker, as his head rattled against the bark of the tree trunks, into which he bored in quest of worms.

The first real surprise of the girl came when she reached the bridge. This proved that she was more than four miles from home, a distance much greater than she had suspected.

"Where can Nick be?" she asked herself, never once thinking that they might have missed each other when she was swinging in the tree-top. It struck her that the day was nearly gone, for she noticed the gathering twilight diffusing itself through the forest.

"I don't think I will go any farther," she said; "Nick will be along pretty soon, and I'll wait here for him."

Standing on the bridge and looking down the road and listening for the sound of the carriage wheels were tiresome to one of Nellie's active habits, and it was not long before she broke off some of the bread, set down her lunch basket, and then dropped some crumbs into the water.

As they struck the surface, sending out little rings toward the shore, several tiny fish came up after the food. Nellie laughed outright, and, in her eagerness, was careless of how she threw the crumbs, most of which fell upon the bank.

It occurred to her that she could do better by going down to the edge of the stream, where she would not mistake her aim.

Childlike, she did not pause to think of the wrong of so doing, for she ought to have known that her parents never would have consented to such an act.

Just there, Nellie, like many another little girl, made a great mistake.

CHAPTER X.

IN GREAT DANGER.

A little child is like a butterfly, thinking only of the pleasures of the moment. Nellie Ribsam came down close to the edge of the creek and threw some crumbs out upon the surface. In the clear water she could see the shadowy figures of the minnows, as they glided upward and snapped at the morsels.

She became so interested in the sport that she kept walking down the bank of the stream, flinging out the crumbs until there was none left in her hand; then she debated whether she should go back after her lunch basket or wait where she was until Nick appeared on the bridge.

"It's a bother to carry the basket with me," she said to herself; "I had to leave it on the ground when I was after grapes, so I'll wait till Nick comes, and then I'll call to him. Won't he be scared when he sees me down here!"

From where she stood, she observed the bridge above her head, and consequently Nick could look directly down upon her whenever he should reach the structure.

Nellie felt that she would like to go on down the creek to the big pond into which it emptied; but she knew better than to do that, for she would be certain to miss her big brother, and it was already beginning to grow dark around her.

"I wonder what makes Nick so long," she said to herself, as she sat down on a fallen tree; "I'm so tired that I never can walk the four miles home."

She had sat thus only a brief while, when her head began to droop; her bright eyes grew dull, then closed, and leaning against a limb which put out from the fallen tree, on which she was sitting, she sank into the sweet, dreamless sleep of childhood and health.

Had she not been disturbed she would not have wakened until the sun rose, but at the end of an hour, an involuntary movement of the head caused it to slip off the limb against which it was resting with such a shock that instantly she was as wide awake as though it was mid-day.

Ah, but when she sprang to her feet and stared about her in the gloom she was dreadfully alarmed!

She was quick-witted enough to understand where she was and how it had all come about. The gibbous moon was directly overhead, and shone down upon her with unobstructed fullness.

"Nick has gone over the bridge while I was asleep," was her instant conclusion; "and father and mother will be worried about me."

Her decision as to what she should do could not but be the one thing—that was to climb back up the bank to the bridge, cross it, and hurry homeward.

There was a little throbbing of the heart, when she reflected that she had several miles to travel, most of which was through the gloomy woods; but there was no hesitation on the part of Nellie, who, but for the sturdy teaching of her parents, would have crouched down beside the log and sobbed in terror until she sank into slumber through sheer exhaustion.

"I have been a bad girl," she said to herself, as she reflected on her thoughtlessness; "and mother will whip me, for I know she ought to; and mother always does what she ought to do."

There was no room for doubt in the mind of the child, for she understood the nature of her parents as well as any child could understand that of its guardian.

Nellie was some distance below the point where the bridge spanned the creek, but she could see the dim outlines of the structure as she started toward it. It seemed higher than usual, but that was because the circumstances were different from any in which she had ever been placed.

The little one was making her way as best she could along the stream in the direction of the bridge, when she was frightened almost out of her senses by hearing a loud, sniffing growl from some point just ahead of her.

It was a sound that would have startled the bravest man, and Nellie was transfixed for the moment. She did not turn and run, nor did she sink in a swoon to the ground, but she stood just where she had stopped, until she could find out what it meant.

She was not kept long in waiting, for in less than a minute the noise was repeated, and at the same moment she caught the outlines of a huge black bear swinging along toward her. He was coming down the bed of the creek, with his awkward, ponderous tread, and when seen by Nellie was within fifty feet of her.

When it is remembered that he was of unusual size and proceeding straight toward the child, it seems impossible that she should have done anything at all to help herself. The sight was enough to deprive her of the power of motion and speech.

But it was in such a crisis as this that little Nellie Ribsam showed that she had not forgotten the teaching of her parents: "God helps them that help themselves."

With scarcely a second's pause, she whirled on her heel and dashed down the stream with the utmost speed at her command.

The bear could not have failed to see her, though it is not to be supposed that he was looking for the little girl when he first came that way. Furthermore, had the chase lasted several minutes Nellie must have fallen a victim to the savage animal.

It required no instruction to teach her that there was but one way in which she could escape, and that was by climbing a tree. Had there been a large one near at hand she would have ascended that as quickly as possible; but, fortunately, the first one to which she fled was a sapling, no larger than those she had climbed during the afternoon, and no one could have clambered to the highest point attainable quicker than did the frightened little girl.

Had she been a veteran hunter, Nellie could not have made a better selection, for she was fully twenty feet from the ground, and as much beyond the reach of the bear as though she were in her trundle-bed at home.

But the position was a frightful one to her, and for several minutes she believed the animal would tear the tree down and destroy her.

"I have done all I can for myself," she murmured, recalling the instruction of her parents, "and now God will do the rest."

Beautiful, trusting faith of childhood! Of such, indeed, is the kingdom of heaven.

The huge bear, which from some cause or other had ventured from the recesses of the wood, was but a short distance behind the little wanderer when she climbed so hastily beyond his reach. He acted as though he was somewhat bewildered by the unusual scene of a small child fleeing from him, but nothing is so tempting to pursuit as the sight of some one running from us, and the brute galloped after Nellie with an evident determination to capture her, if the thing could be done.

When he found the child had eluded him for the time, he sat down on his haunches and looked upward, as though he intended to wait till she would be compelled to descend and surrender herself.

The small tree in which Nellie had taken refuge was several yards from the edge of the stream, the bank sloping so steeply that the water never reached the base, excepting during a freshet.

It was a chestnut, whose smooth bark rendered it all the more difficult to climb, but Nellie went up it as rapidly as a man ascends telegraph poles with the spikes strapped to his boots.

The bear clawed the bark a little while, as a cat is sometimes seen to do when "stretching" herself, and it was during these few minutes that the girl thought nothing could save her from falling into his clutches.

When he ceased, she peered downward through the branches, and could just see the massy animal near the base of the tree, as if asking himself what was the next best thing to do.

It will be admitted that the situation of Nellie Ribsam was one in which few children of her tender years are ever placed. Happy it is, indeed, that it is so, for what one in a thousand would have retained her self-possession?

In explanation, it may be doubted indeed whether Nellie fully comprehended her peril. Had she been older, her consternation, doubtless, would have been greater, as the emotion she showed some years later, when placed in great danger, would seem to prove.

But there was one fact of which she was firmly convinced: she had complied with her father's instructions, for, as has been shown, she put forth every possible exertion to save herself, and now she called on Heaven to assist her.

Perched in the top of the tree, with the enormous bear sitting beneath and looking hungrily upward, she prayed:

"Heavenly Father, please take care of me and don't let that big bear catch me; don't let papa and mamma feel too bad, and please make the bad bear go away and let me alone."

CHAPTER XI.

"GOTT SEI DANK!"

The prayer of little Nellie Ribsam—so far as it related to herself—was answered.

She secured her seat, as best she could, in the branches of the chestnut sapling, and, by arranging her dress and the yielding limbs with considerable skill, she made herself quite comfortable.

The trying situation in which she was placed, it would be thought, was enough to drive away all disposition to sleep, but at the end of less than half an hour the little head was nodding again, and, forgetful of her peril, her senses soon left her.

It will be understood that the danger of the young wanderer was rendered all the greater by this loss of consciousness, for her muscles would relax in slumber, and, unless her position was unusually secure, she was certain to fall.

But that gracious Father in whom she so implicitly trusted watched over the little one, and she remained as though seated in the broad rocking-chair at home.

When at last she moved slightly and was on the point of losing her balance, she awoke so quickly that she saved herself just in the nick of time.

She was shocked and startled, but regaining her breath she held fast with one hand while she parted the branches with the other and carefully peered down among the limbs.

"He is gone!" was her joyous exclamation; "I knew the Lord would make him go away, because I asked him to."

She was right: the bear had vanished, and all danger from that source for the time had passed.

The brute probably found enough to eat without waiting for little girls to fall into his clutches. As he had never been known to trouble any one in the neighborhood, it was reasonable to believe that he got all he wanted without venturing away from the depths of the woods, and rousing an ill-will against himself that would speedily result in his destruction.

Nellie did not feel surprised at all, for, as I have shown, she had the faith to believe that her prayer would be answered.

"Now I will go down to the ground and start for home. I guess the bear isn't far off, but the Lord will not let him hurt me."

She carefully descended the tree and stood on the ground a minute later. She found that her dress was torn and she had lost part of the ribbon from her hat. This troubled her more than anything else, for her frugal mother had told her many a time that she must take the best care of her clothing.

"I was so scared that I forgot to look out," she said to herself, after taking an inventory of the damages; "but I guess mother will excuse me for losing the ribbon, though I know she won't for coming so far into the woods without permission."

She now set out resolutely for the bridge, determined to lose no more time in reaching home. As is the rule, the brief space she had passed in sleep seemed three times as long as was actually the case, and she thought it must be near morning.

She had gone but a short distance when she stopped with another shock of affright.

"My gracious! what can that be?"

A point of light appeared between her and the bridge, flickering about like an *ignis-fatuus* or jack-o'-lantern. Nellie felt like taking to the tree again, but she bravely stood her ground until she could satisfy her curiosity as to its nature.

Watching it closely she observed shadowy figures flitting around the light in a curious and grotesque way. She was in greater doubt than ever, when she heard voices.

"I think I saw her tracks, but I couldn't be sure; Nellie knows too much to walk or fall into the deep water."

"I hope so, but my heart misgives me sorely. God be merciful, for if she is lost I can never recover!"

The first speaker was Nick Ribsam, and the second was the father, the mother immediately adding:

"Why the poor child came here is more than I can understand, but He doeth all things well."

"Oh, mother! Oh, father! Oh, Nick! It is I, Nellie! I am so glad to see you!"

And the little wanderer flew like the wind along the bank of the creek. The mother was the first to recognize the voice, and rushing forward she caught her child in her arms, murmuring in her own language:

"Mein Kind! Mein Kind! Gott sei Dank!" (My child! My child! God be thanked!)

"Mein lieber Nellie! Komm an mein Herz! Kannst du es sein?" (My dear Nellie! Come to my heart! Can it be you?) exclaimed the overjoyed father.

"O meine abtrünnige Schwester! Wie du uns erschreckt hast! Wie es mich freut dich zu finden!" (Oh, my truant sister! What a scare you have given us! How glad I am to find you!) shouted Nick.

And the child that was lost and was found was hugged first by mother, then by father, and then by Nick, and then all strove to get hold of her at the same time, till the brother ceased, through fear that she would be torn apart.

Nellie was laughing and crying, and wondering why it was such commotion was caused by her return to her folks.

Mr. Layton and Kilgore heard the tumult, and knew what it meant. A few minutes brought them to the spot, and, though their greeting was less demonstrative, their eyes filled with tears over the exceeding joy of the reunited family.

When the excitement had subsided somewhat, the group listened to the story of Nellie. She told it in her childish, straightforward manner, and it was all the more impressive on that account.

The listeners were greatly touched; but the probability that a large bear was in the neighborhood hastened their footsteps and they lost no time in hurrying away.

When they reached the highway above, crossed the bridge, and had gone some distance on their way home, they began to feel there was nothing to be feared from the animal. Mr. Layton referred to the tracks of the beast which they had noticed when hunting for Nellie, but said he would never have mentioned it until the fate of the girl became known; for the suggestions which must have followed were too dreadful.

Nothing was seen of the animal, however, and, as the distance from the bridge was increased the party finally gave up all thought and conversation respecting it.

There was a grateful household that night, when, at a late hour, they gathered about the family altar and the head returned thanks to Him who had been so merciful to them and theirs.

The happy mother held the daughter in her arms all night, while they both slept; and when the parent awoke, now and then, through the darkness, she shuddered, pressed the little one closer to her and kissed the chubby cheek, on which her former tears had not yet dried.

But Katrina Ribsam was none the less an affectionate mother when, several days later, she called Nellie to her knee and told her how wrongly she had acted in venturing on such a dangerous tramp without asking permission from her parents.

Nellie said she knew it, and wondered why it was her mother delayed the punishment so long. She was ready, and loved and respected her mother the more for administering it.

But truth compels me to say that the chastisement was given with such a gentle hand that it was hardly worth the name, and the mother herself suffered far more than did the child, who to this day is not conscious that she received anything like physical pain.

CHAPTER XII.

OMINOUS PREPARATIONS.

Happily there are few little girls in this favored land who are called upon to go through such trials as fell to the lot of little Nellie Ribsam when she was but eight years old.

It created much talk in the neighborhood, and she was complimented on the bravery she had shown, while the glad father became more confirmed than ever in his favorite belief that God helps them that help themselves.

"'Spose dot she didn't try to helps herself some," he said, in talking the matter over with Mr. Marston, "don't you not sees dot she would get eat up doo, dree times by dot bear dot vos bigger as nefer vos?"

"It is a good thing for one, even though he be a child, to be able to do his utmost when overtaken by danger—there can be no question about *that*; but it would require a great deal of training to bring some children to that point, even when they are double the years of your little girl."

"Dot's becos dere folks don't not begins right; we starts mit Nick and Nellie when dey was so small dot dey didn't know nuffin, which is why it happens dey knows so much now."

Great as was the interest excited by the adventure of Nellie, it was not long before it was thrown in the shade by another fact which was brought to light by that same experience: that was the existence of a large bear in the woods which lay to the east and west of the road leading to Dunbarton.

This forest, as has already been intimated, covered a large tract of country, in which, a few years previous, bears, deer, and wolves had been hunted by many of those dwelling on the outskirts. Large inroads had been made on the woodland, and here and there the cabin of a settler or squatter was found by those who penetrated any distance.

There were clearings extending over several acres, while, again, a man might wander for hours without emerging from the timber, which included the common varieties found in the Middle States—oak, beech, maple, birch, hickory, hemlock, black walnut, American poplar or whitewood, gum, elm, persimmon, and others less important.

The pine resembled the famous white pine of the Allegheny mountains, and predominated. Where there was such a large area covered with timber, about every variety of surface was known. In some places were rocks, ravines, hollows, and gulches; in others there were marshy swamps through which a hunter would find it hard work to force his way.

Shark Creek entered from the east and was of considerable volume. In many places it was deep, while elsewhere it widened into broad and shallow expansions. It wound its way through the woods in the sinuous course always taken by such streams, and, crossing the road, where it was spanned by a bridge, it continued onward a quarter of a mile, when it reached Shark Pond, the overflow of which ultimately found its way into the Susquehanna and so to the Atlantic.

Why the waters were called Shark Creek and Pond was more than any one could explain. Most likely it was because no such fish as the shark had ever been seen near them, the circumstances of the case rendering it impossible that such a voracious creature ever should have sported in their depths.

From what has been said, it will be seen that the woods offered a most inviting home for a few wild bears, and there was the best reason for the belief of many of the neighbors that if the tract was well hunted over several of the animals would be found.

The universal opinion was that they should be exterminated, for so long as they were in the woods, so long were they a standing menace to all the men, women, and children who dwelt in the section. The children, especially, were considered in great peril, and several timid mothers refused to let their girls and boys go to school, which stood at no great distance from the woods.

There was more than one farmer who contended that, if the few bears were left alone they would multiply to that degree that they would sally forth from the forest, like the Delaware Indians of the last century, and carry death and destruction before them.

A few individuals, like Gustav Ribsam, said there was nothing to fear, for when the bears showed any marked increase they would be killed, and it would be no very difficult job, either.

But no one could dispute the desirability of ridding the country of the brute which came so near eating little Nellie Ribsam; and, where there was so much talk, something was done, or at least attempted.

A hunting party of six men was organized in the month of October, and they tramped through the woods for days, with a couple of dogs, but the trail of the animal could not be found. They finally gave up the hunt, the most tired and disgusted not hesitating to declare they did not believe a bear had been seen in the forest for half a century.

The opinion of those best qualified to judge, was that bruin obtained all the food he wanted with such little trouble that he did not care to molest any persons, and therefore kept out of the way of the hunters.

Nick Ribsam, like all boys, was fond of a gun and dog, and he did not own either. His father had brought from Holland an old musket, used before the country was erected into a kingdom for Louis Bonaparte, more than eighty years ago; but when Nick rammed a charge down its dusty throat one day, forgetful that one had been resting there for months, and pulled trigger, it hung fire a long time; but, when it did go off, it did so in an overwhelming fashion, bursting into a dozen pieces and narrowly missing killing the astounded lad who discharged it.

But Nick was so anxious to own a gun, that his father bought him one on the day he reached the age of ten years, which was shortly after Nellie's adventure with the bear. Although the farmer was frugal in all things, he believed it was the cheapest to buy the best, and the gun which was placed in the hands of Nick was a breech-loader with double barrels. It was a shot-gun, as a matter of course, for little use could be found for a rifle in that neighborhood.

But Nick had practiced with this piece only a few weeks, when his ambition was turned in another direction by a large, strong boy, who hired himself out upon the farm of Mr. Marston. He was sixteen years of age, and was named Sam Harper. His father had been a soldier in the late war, and gave to Sam a fine breech-loading rifle, which he brought with him when he hired out to Mr. Marston.

The lad had owned it two years, and, under the tutelage of his father, who was wounded and living upon a pension, he became very skillful for one of his age.

Beside this, Mr. Marston himself, as I have shown, was fond of hunting in his early manhood, and was the owner of an excellent muzzle-loading rifle, which was as good as when his keen eye glanced along the brown barrel and the bullet was buried in the unsuspicious deer, so far away as to be scarcely visible to the ordinary vision.

"If you and Sam want to hunt the bear," said the kind owner, "you are welcome to my rifle, for you know a shot-gun ain't exactly the thing to go hunting bears with."

"That's just what I want it for," said Nick, with sparkling eyes.

CHAPTER XIII.

THE BEAR HUNTERS.

Nothing is impossible to pluck and perseverance. That boy who is determined to become brilliant in his studies, no matter what their nature, or to master a difficult profession, or to attain any point possible of attainment, is sure to win, if he will but *stick to it*.

Nick Ribsam was resolved to become skillful with the rifle, and he gave all the time he could spare to practice with the gun which belonged to Mr. Marston. He was desirous of starting after the bear with Sam, as soon as he could use the gun, but his sensible father shook his head.

"No, Nicholas, that would be doing wrong, for you do not know how to handle the rifle; God does not step in and help the lazy and careless; first learn how to use the weapon, so you will never miss; then you may go hunt bears."

Although a lusty lad, Nick found the heavy gun was quite a burden, and he preferred to rest the barrel on the fence, or in the crotch of a tree, when aiming, but Sam Harper told him he could never amount to anything unless he used his weapon off-hand, and was ready to do so effectively, no matter how sudden the call.

Nick applied all his energies, and in the course of a few weeks won the praise of Sam, who had become very fond of the bright and good-natured "Pennsylvania Dutchman," who, in return, helped him in his efforts to improve his knowledge in arithmetic, which he studied in a desultory way on the long autumn evenings, having promised his father to do so.

Mr. Marston owned a dog which was not of much account, but the boys trained him with rare patience, and were confident he would prove valuable when they took him on the hunt.

By the time they were ready to start autumn was advanced, and Nick, who had carefully studied up the peculiarities of the animal, said he was afraid the bear had gone into some hollow tree or cave to take his winter's sleep.

"I don't think they do that till the weather gets colder," said Sam, who had once helped hunt bruin in the wilds of Tennessee, "and even in very cold weather I have seen their tracks in the snow; but if we can only find the tree or cave where he is hiding, why, that will just be splendid."

"Why so?"

"He is fat, lazy, and so sleepy that he don't fight much; but in the spring-time he is lean, hungry, and fierce, and then everybody must look out. There are so many chestnuts and hickory nuts in the woods now that he can get all he wants to eat without scaring the farmers by visiting them."

"The bear eats almost everything," said Nick, "but I don't believe he can make much of a meal off hickory nuts."

"Well, he has got a good thing of it anyway, here, there is so much food around him, and if he had only been smart enough to keep out of sight and never show himself he might have died of old age without being once disturbed by hunters."

"I ain't sure he won't die of old age as it is," said Nick, with a laugh; "for every one who went after him came back without the first glimpse. I guess they have all given up hope of shooting him, and I shouldn't wonder if we had to do the same."

But whether such was to be the result or not remained to be seen, and the boys were sure of plenty of sport in an all-day ramble through the woods.

During all this time Nick and Nellie were attending school, and they maintained their places in their studies, and were surpassed by none in the excellence of their deportment.

Nick rose early and helped his father with his work, and at night did his chores. With all this, he found opportunity to practice with the rifle and to prepare his lessons for the morrow, so that it need not be said he had little idle time on his hands.

On a bright Saturday morning in November, when the smoky haze of the delicious Indian summer overspread forest, stream, and country, Sam Harper came to the house of Nick Ribsam according to appointment.

His rifle was slung over his shoulder, and the dog, which they had christened Bowser, was at his heels. There was no school that day, and Mr. Ribsam, having satisfied himself of the ability of Nick to handle the rifle of his neighbor, had given him permission to go on a hunt for the bear which had so frightened Nellie a couple of months before.

The mother and daughter were a little anxious when the rosy-cheeked boy donned his heavy boots, pushed his trousers down the legs, and taking the long-barreled rifle from where it rested in the corner turned to kiss them good-by.

Mr. Ribsam seemed as cool and stolid as ever; but any one looking closely at him would have observed that he puffed his pipe a little oftener than was his wont, while his eye beamed more kindly upon his brave little boy.

"Look out, Nick, and don't be too venturesome," said the mother, as she pressed her lips to those of her only son.

"And remember that the bear is an awful big animal," said Nellie, "for I *seen* him."

The brother, who was in the act of leaning over his sister to kiss her, drew back with a reproving look.

"Why is it a girl can't talk without saying 'awful' in every sentence? I wish for variety's sake, Nellie, you and the rest of the girls would leave 'awful' out of one sentence in a hundred, and don't say 'I *seen* him,' for you know better than that, sister."

She hung her head and her eyes were growing misty, when Nick took the kiss with a laugh and moved to the door.

"There, there, good-by; you all act as if I was going to Africa to hunt lions and tigers."

Nellie snapped him up in a flash:

"There ain't any tigers in Africa, smarty!"

"You got me that time," laughed Nick; "where is father?"

"He went out of the door a minute ago; he is standing by the gate," said the mother, after a quick glance through the window.

Mr. Ribsam was leaning on the gate-post, as was a favorite custom of his, and the tobacco smoke ascended in clouds and rings, as though he was a locomotive tugging hard at a train, with the wheels continually slipping.

He looked at the boys without stirring or speaking, as they passed out the gate and gently closed it, so as not to jar the old gentleman leaning upon it.

When they had gone a rod or so, Mr. Ribsam called out:

"Nicholas!"

"Yes, sir!" answered the son, wheeling instantly.

The father took the long stem of his pipe from his mouth, emitted a blast of vapor, and then shut his eyes and flung his head backward with a quick flirt, which meant that his boy should come to him.

Nick obeyed with his usual promptness, and paused immediately in front of his parent, while Sam Harper stopped short and looked backward at the two, with the purpose of waiting until the interview ended.

The old gentleman meant his words for both, and he therefore used the English tongue as best he could, and spoke loud:

"Nicholas, bears ish shtrong amimals as nefer vos: they can squeeze in der ribs of a ox of dey tried, I dinks, so looks out dot de bears don't not squeeze mit you."

"I will take good care, you may depend."

"His claws am sharp and he has big jaws; look outs for dem, Nicholas!"

"You may be sure I will."

"And, Nicholas, ven you goes for to hunt bears *you must helps one anoder; you hears?*"

This was the all-important sentence the father had prepared himself to utter. It will be observed that it was in violation of his oft repeated creed, for it clearly called upon the boys to render mutual support should danger arise; and they would have been zanies had they not done so.

The father expected them to show that much sense, but he was impelled to impress the necessity of it: he meant them to understand that his declarations were subject to amendment under certain conditions.

Nick gave the pledge and stepped briskly up the road with Sam, while Bowser frolicked in the fields and road until they were fairly in the woods, when he frisked among the trees, sometimes starting up a squirrel or rabbit, which had no trouble in skurrying out of his reach.

As the bear when seen by Nellie was near Shark Creek, the boys agreed to follow the road to the bridge, descend into the bed of the stream, and then go downward toward the pond and finally off into the woods, where they intended to pass that day and probably the night and following day.

They had reached and passed the tree in which Nellie Ribsam took refuge two months before, when Nick suddenly exclaimed:

"Hallo, there is some one ahead of us!"

"It's the season for game and we shall find plenty of hunters in the wood," said Sam Harper, who, nevertheless, scanned the person with much interest.

The fact that the boys were following precisely in his footsteps raised the suggestion that perhaps he was engaged on the same business or sport, as it might be termed.

Our friends hastened their pace so as to overtake him, for his company might be desirable, or possibly it might be otherwise.

"Hallo, there!" called out Nick; "wait a minute!"

The individual thus hailed turned about, and looked back to see who it was that called.

As he did so his face was seen, and Nick Ribsam gave utterance to an expression of astonishment.

CHAPTER XIV.

A RECRUIT.

The stranger ahead of the two boys was Herbert Watrous, the city youth upon whom Nick had sat down so hard three years before.

He was unusually tall when visiting the country school, and during the intervening time he had continued to grow upward, until his height equaled that of an ordinary man. He was scarce fourteen years old, but he lacked very little of six feet in altitude.

He was correspondingly slim, so that he looked as if a smart blow on the back would snap him in two. He was arrayed in a most gorgeous hunting suit of green, with all the paraphernalia which the hunter from the city thinks necessary when he honors the country with a tramp for game.

Herbert, beyond question, was fitted out in fine style, and there was nothing lacking, except perhaps skill. He carried one of the finest of breech-loading rifles, which would have been very effective in the hands of a party who knew how to use it.

The face of the lad had not changed in expression to any extent since Nick Ribsam drove him into the earth, but there was some downy furze on his upper lip and chin, while his voice was of that squeaky and uncertain tone heard when "changing."

"Hallo! is that you?" was the rather superfluous question of Herbert, as he waited for the two boys to come up. He recognized Nick, but of course was a stranger to Sam Harper, to whom Nick introduced him, and there was a general shaking of hands all around.

Young Watrous glanced rather askance at his old school-mate, but there was such a cordial welcome on the part of the young "American of Dutch descent" that all reserve vanished.

A certain loftiness of manner and conceit of expression, however, were natural to Herbert, and he did not fail to look down, in a literal and figurative sense, upon the two hunters.

"That's a fine gun you have there, Herbert," said Nick, venturing to reach out his hand for it.

"Yes," answered Herbert, passing it to him rather gingerly, "be careful not to drop it."

The gun was a beautiful weapon, known as the long range "Creedmoor." It was a Remington, highly finished, and cost $125. It had a front sight, known as the wind-gauge, with the spirit-level, and with the vernier sight on the stock, which is raised from its flat position when the hunter wishes to shoot a long distance, and is graduated up to a thousand yards, carrying a 44 cartridge.

"That isn't of much account in this part of the world," said Sam Harper, passing the weapon back; "it's light enough, for I don't suppose it weighs more than six or seven pounds."

"It's just the thing for these woods," said Herbert, in his important manner, "for I calculate to bring down game a half mile away, if I happen to see it."

"And provided it will stand still and you can know the exact distance."

"I can tell that by my eye easily enough."

"You can't guess within two hundred yards of it, if your life depended on it."

"That remains to be seen."

"The first time you try it will prove it. I have seen them shoot with the telescopes, globe, and peep sights and all the new fangled notions, and they're good only for fancy shooting. You've got to use that breech-loader off-hand, just as I do, or it won't be worth a cent to you."

"I understand that a big black bear has been seen in the woods," said Herbert, in his loftiest style; "I've come to kill him."

Nick and Sam looked significantly at each other, and Nick said:

"That is what we are after; won't you join us?"

Instead of responding promptly, Herbert said:

"Well, I don't know as I have any objection to letting you go with me, though you must promise to do as I say."

Without giving this pledge, the two said they would render all the help they could, and the party moved on down the creek toward the pond.

"Have you a dog?" asked Nick of their new recruit.

"No, what do I want of a dog? He would only be a bother; you ought to send back that pumpkin of yours."

"We don't expect him to be of much help, except to find the track of the bear, if he is anywhere in the neighborhood—*there!* do you hear that?"

At that moment Bowser, who had trotted into the woods ahead, gave utterance to a hoarse, resounding bay, which sounded as though his voice had also changed, for it ended in a dismal squeaking howl that made all laugh.

"He is on the track of something," said Nick in some excitement.

"A rabbit, I am sure," remarked Herbert, with a sneer.

The three started off at a rapid walk, which occasionally broke into a trot, and following the baying of the hound they turned to the right before reaching the big pond, and struck into the very heart of the woods.

Herbert was so much taller and lighter than his companions that he drew away from them once or twice, but was obliging enough to stop and wait.

Hurrying along in this headlong fashion they soon stopped, all pretty well out of breath.

Although Herbert had laughed at their tardiness, he was the most exhausted and the first one to wish to rest.

CHAPTER XV.

A SURPRISE.

All this time the baying of the hound continued, the sounds showing that he had circled and was approaching the boys, who were not a little astonished at the unexpected turn of affairs.

"That's a pretty dog," laughed Herbert; "he is making fools of us all."

"There isn't any need of that so far as *you* are concerned," retorted Nick, losing patience with the slurs of their companion. "You had better wait till you find out what it means before you condemn Bowser."

Herbert made no answer, for the dog was now so close that the interest of all was centered on his actions.

"My gracious, what a terrible racket he makes!" exclaimed Nick; "there must be something unusual to excite Bowser like that."

The dog was not heard for several minutes, but the crashing through the undergrowth sounded nearer and nearer, and, as Sam declared, showed that Bowser had steam up and was going for something.

Suddenly the bushes parted only a short ways from where the three wondering lads stood, and, instead of the hound, some kind of a wild animal came toward them on a dead run.

The group were too amazed to think of the guns they held, and only stared in mute wonder.

The game did not see them until within a hundred feet, when he whirled at right angles and plunged away with arrowy speed.

As he did so, he exposed his flank to the young hunters, who could not have been given a better opportunity to bring him down, for the throwing forward of the foreleg, opened his most vulnerable part to the bullet.

But none was sent after him; at that instant he was recognized as a fine buck deer, with branching antlers thrown back so that they seemed to rest on his spine, while his legs were flung straight in front and then backward, as he took his long graceful leaps.

The boys had set out to hunt a bear, and were astounded that, when they dared not hope they were anywhere in his vicinity, a splendid deer should spring up and dash by them.

Before they could give utterance to their amazement, Bowser came along with his nose to the ground and baying hoarsely.

Just as he turned to follow the deer, Herbert Watrous raised his breech-loader to his shoulder and fired point blank at him.

"What did you do that for?" demanded Sam Harper, striding threateningly toward him with his fist raised.

"Why—why—I declare! I thought it was the bear!" exclaimed the abashed Herbert; "I never dreamed it was the dog."

Sam was not disposed to believe this story, and he stood irresolute, strongly inclined to punish the city youth who had fired at his hound; but Nick compelled his angry friend to laugh by saying:

"You shouldn't be mad, Sam, for Bowser is safe so long as Herbert aims at him. I don't think he came within twenty feet. If he should hit him you can make up your mind it is an accident."

Herbert hardly knew how to answer this remark, for he saw that he had not done a very creditable thing, view it as he might, so he made a radical turn in the conversation.

"Who would have thought it, boys? We've got not only a bear, but a deer to hunt, and I say, may the best fellow win!"

And with this manly sentiment on his lips he broke into a rapid run after the buck and hound, the others following, forgetful of the little flurry a few minutes before.

It was not in the order of things that the lads should be able to make their way through the woods and undergrowth with anything like the speed of the fallow deer or dog. Hunters don't expect to overtake their game in anything like a fair chase when all are on foot, but resort to stratagem.

By stationing themselves so as to head off a deer, they secure the one shot which is all-sufficient. It would be counted an extremely good piece of fortune could they obtain such a fair target as has already been given the young hunters; and, having let it pass unimproved, they scarcely would have expected to be so favored again.

It was natural, therefore, that they should make a pell-mell rush after the deer and hound, and that they should keep going until, once more, they were forced to stop from exhaustion.

By this time the baying of Bowser came to them so faintly that it was plain he was a mile distant at the least, while there could be little doubt that the buck was much farther off.

"Well!" exclaimed the panting Herbert Watrous, "I can't say I see much fun in this; it's too much like chasing a railroad train."

"No," added Nick, "I don't see that there is any hope of running down the deer, who is more used to traveling than we are."

"Maybe he'll come round in a circle again," said Sam, "and we may have another chance to see him sail by, while not one of us raises his gun."

"I suppose we ought to understand something more about the habits of the deer, so that we would know what course he would be likely to take. We could then get there ahead of him and fire as soon as he gave us a chance."

"Well," added Sam, with a sigh, "he seems to have taken the route we were going to follow to hunt the bear, so we may as well tramp along. We may get a glimpse of a buffalo or elephant next."

The baying of the hound had ceased, and, though the boys often stopped and listened, they heard nothing more of it.

"I guess he has caught the deer," said Herbert, who showed a desire to speak well of Bowser since he had failed to shoot him, "and is waiting for us."

But Sam shook his head; he knew the canine too well to believe him capable of such an exploit as that.

"I don't think he ever ran down anything yet, unless it was a chicken or cat— hallo!"

At that moment the subject of their conversation appeared on the scene, approaching as quietly as though the boys were sheep that he wished to surprise.

He slouched along with a lazy, tired gait, his tongue out, and dripping with perspiration, while he panted as though he had been on the severest chase of his life, which most likely was the fact.

He lay down at the feet of Sam Harper, and, stretching out his paws, rested his head between them as much as to say, "Gentlemen, I have had enough of this sport, and resign; you will now carry it on without my assistance."

"He is tired out, and I don't wonder," said Sam, stooping over and patting the head of the hound; "he ain't used to deer hunting, and don't know much more about it than do we."

"Then he don't know anything," was the truthful observation of Nick Ribsam.

"It's my opinion that it's best to give up hunting that particular deer until we learn a little more about the right way to do it."

CHAPTER XVI.

THE DINNER IN THE WOODS.

By this time it was close to the hour of noon, and the young hunters were hungry. They had brought no lunch with them, for that would have been an admission that they doubted their own ability to provide food for themselves in a country abounding with game.

Nick Ribsam had a paper of salt and pepper mixed, with which to season their dinner as soon as it should be secured.

The common red squirrels, or chickarees, were so plentiful that they were nearly always in sight, and, without moving from where they stood, the lads descried several running along the limbs of the trees.

"Let each of us shoot one," said Sam, walking forth to get a better aim at a fellow perched high on the branch of a large oak.

Slowly bringing his gun to his shoulder, he took careful aim, and the game came tumbling through the leaves to the ground, his head punctured by the cruel bullet. Bowser started at a lazy walk to bring the body in, but Sam stopped him and picked it up himself.

"I think I will take *that* one," said Herbert, indicating a squirrel which was nearer than the others. It was sitting in the crotch of a tree, nigh enough to be struck with a stone flung by a skillful thrower.

The other two watched his actions with some interest as he raised the handsome breech-loader. He took a long and deliberate aim, and gave a grunt the instant he pulled the trigger, and the sharp report broke the stillness of the woods.

Nick and Sam laughed, for the frightened rodent scampered up the tree and ran out upon a heavy branch, where he whisked from sight and then back again, chattering in such a lively fashion that it was plain he had suffered no inconvenience from the bullet sent after him.

"Well, I'll be hanged!" exclaimed the chagrined Herbert, "I don't understand how that came about."

"The squirrel doesn't seem to understand it, either," said Sam; "let's see whether you can do any worse, Nick."

"I'm going to try and bark him," remarked Nick, cocking his rifle and sighting at the little animal.

Before he could make his aim sure, the chickaree started to run along the limb, which was large and covered with thick, shaggy bark; but the muzzle of the weapon swerved slowly in a corresponding direction, and just as the game gathered itself to make a leap, the explosion came.

The others, who were watching the squirrel to note the result, saw several pieces of bark suddenly fly upward with such force that the rodent was hurled fully a foot above the limb, dropping like a wet rag at the feet of the lad, killed, without its skin being broken.

"That was a good shot!" exclaimed Sam Harper admiringly; "no hunter in the land could have barked him better than did you."

"What do you mean by barking a squirrel?" asked Herbert, who had never seen anything of the kind before.

"It is easy enough; all you have to do is to cut the bark right under the squirrel's body, so that the pieces fly upward with such force as to knock the life from him."

"That's the way I'm going to kill them after this."

"It is best to practice hitting them with the ball first," Nick suggested.

Herbert solemnly removed the shell of the cartridge from his breech-loader and replaced it with a fresh one, pretending not to hear the remark of Nick.

As the two squirrels were large and in excellent condition, it was thought they would afford enough dinner for the boys, who went some distance farther until they reached a small stream of clear, icy water, where they decided to make their fire.

While Nick and Herbert busied themselves gathering some dry twigs and sticks, Sam Harper, with his keen knife, skillfully skinned the chickarees, dressed them, and then holding them over the flame on green, forked sticks, they were soon cooked to a turn.

For a few minutes before they were ready, the odor of the broiling game so sharpened the appetites of the boys that Nick sprang up, and, hurrying out in the woods, shot another for Sam to dress and cook.

"Two ain't enough," he said in explanation, as he threw the last to his friend; "I can eat a couple myself, and Bowser looks sort of faint."

"The waste parts ought to be enough for him," said Sam, glancing at the hound, who had gulped down everything thrown him and was gazing wistfully for the next tid-bits that should fall to his share.

The clear, pure air, the vigorous exercise, and the rugged health of the boys gave them appetites scarcely less forceful than that of Bowser; and when Nick had carefully sprinkled the seasoning over the juicy, crisp flesh, and each, taking one of the squirrels in hand, began wrenching off the tender meat, he was sure he had never tasted such a delicious dinner in all his life.

Even Herbert Watrous, accustomed as he was to the delicacies and refinements of a city home, admitted that there was something about the meal which, washed down with clear, pure water, had a flavor surpassing anything of the kind he had ever known.

The causes why it tasted thus I have already stated.

CHAPTER XVII.

A TEST OF MARKSMANSHIP.

The boys were so tired from their severe tramp, and the rest was so grateful after finishing their dinner, that they stayed where they were an hour longer. Then, realizing that nothing could be done by idleness, they slung their reloaded rifles over their shoulders, took another drink of water, and lazily made their way to higher ground.

"I have been thinking," said Nick, when they paused again, "that we will be more likely to learn something of the bear if we separate."

"For how long?" Herbert asked.

"Until night, or until we find him."

"But how can we find each other at night?"

"That can be fixed easily enough; if necessary, we can signal to each other, or we can pick out some landmark that can be seen a long ways off and gradually approach that as the sun goes down."

There was nothing brilliant in this proposition, but after some discussion it was agreed to by the others, and they began looking around for something which might serve them as a guide.

Directly to the north, the woods rose in a series of hills of no great elevation, but among them were numerous large rocks of limestone formation, some of them of such a light color that they could be seen a long distance.

"Right yonder," said Nick, pointing toward the largest, "is one which we cannot mistake; let's agree to meet there at nightfall and go into camp. If either one of us loses his reckoning he will fire his gun and the others will answer him, so there need be no danger at all."

"I don't see as there would be any danger if we failed to find each other before morning," said Sam; "we are not in a wild country where Indians will hunt for us."

"There ain't any danger," said Herbert, "only it will be a great deal more pleasant to spend the night together; you will feel safer by knowing that I am with you with my patent breech-loader."

"Yes," said Nick, "for by keeping close to you there won't be half as much likelihood of being hit when you fire at something else."

"I haven't tried yet," said Herbert; "my gun is a long-distance shooter: there's where I get my work in. Show me a mark a good long distance off and you'll open your eyes."

"Well, I declare, if that doesn't beat all!"

It was Sam Harper who uttered this exclamation. He had been gazing steadily at a broad, flat rock about a quarter of a mile distant to the northwest of them, and his words announced that he had made some important discovery.

The peculiar tone in which he spoke caused the others to turn toward him and ask the cause.

"Look at that yellowish white rock," he answered, pointing toward it, "and tell me whether that isn't a little ahead of anything yet."

One brief searching glance showed that the young man had sufficient cause for his excitement.

"Now I'll show you what my Creedmoor will do," said Herbert Watrous.

Standing on the top of the rock, so that his figure was thrown in clear relief against the tinted sky behind him, was the very buck they had been vainly chasing. He seemed to be looking back at the young hunters as though he disdained their prowess and defied them to renew their attempt to bring him down.

"That's my chance!" exclaimed Herbert, in excitement; "that's just my

distance; get out of my way! give me room! now I'll show you what my Creedmoor will do, when aimed by a master of the art."

With great display and ceremony the youth prepared to give an exhibition of shooting like that shown at the international matches. The others stepped back, so as not to impede his movements, and he deliberately threw off his cap, got down on his back, raised the rear sight, crossed his feet and drew them half way up to his body, then rested the barrel of his gun on the support thus furnished between the knees, and with his left hand beneath his head, and turned so as to rest against the stock of his gun, while his right was crooked around with the finger lightly pressing the trigger, he was in the proper position to make a "crack shot."

The others watched his actions with the closest attention, only fearful that the deer would not keep his position long enough for Herbert to obtain the aim he wished.

The conditions could not have been more favorable; the buck being to the northwest, while the sun was high in the heavens, there was no confusion of vision from that cause. The smokiness of the atmosphere was so slight that it was scarcely perceptible at so brief a distance, while there was not the least breath of air stirring.

"I am afraid he will lose his chance if he waits too long," said Nick impatiently, in an undertone to Sam, who whispered back:

"The buck understands him and will wait."

It was evident that Mr. Herbert Watrous did not mean to spoil his aim by haste. Shutting one eye, he squinted carefully through his sights, lowering or raising the stock or barrel so as to shift the aim, until at last he had it elevated and pointed to suit him.

Sam watched the buck, while Nick kept his eye on the marksman, who was holding his breath, with his finger crowding the trigger harder and harder until the explosion came.

As before, Herbert uttered a grunt the instant the piece was discharged, and then, hastily clambering to his feet, he put on his cap and said with the utmost assurance:

"That bullet struck him in the chest and will be found buried in his body."

"He doesn't know you fired at him," said Sam Harper, as the buck, a moment later, turned about and walked out of sight.

"The deer doesn't fall at once, even if you drive the bullet through his heart. That buck may go a hundred yards or so, but he will then drop as if struck by lightning."

The confidence with which these words were uttered puzzled Nick and caused him to think that possibly the boaster was right after all, and he had made the shot he claimed.

The truth would probably be learned during the afternoon, for Nick meant to learn it for himself.

Now that they agreed to separate, it was decided that Herbert should keep straight along the route they had been following. Sam should diverge to the right, while Nick would swerve far enough to the left to pass the rock whereupon the buck stood at the time he was shot or rather shot at.

"I am bound to find out the truth," said Nick, with a shake of the head.

And so he did; but little did he dream of what was to happen to him during this search for the truth.

CHAPTER XVIII.

A QUAIL.

As the hound belonged to Sam Harper and showed a disposition to go with him, he was allowed to do so, the lad moving off to the right and Nick Ribsam to the left, as was agreed upon.

Nick had not his father's watch with him, but Herbert Watrous carried a handsome gold hunting-piece, which was now consulted and showed it was nearly two o'clock.

"The days are getting short," said Sam Harper, with a doubtful shake of the head; "that doesn't leave us more than three hours of daylight, and it is hardly worth while to part company."

"What's the odds?" laughed Nick, who was anxious to look for the deer; "we won't be far apart, as we may be to-morrow."

And, without waiting to discuss the question, he struck to the left with his strong step, the others following the courses already mentioned.

No afternoon could have been more charming, with the summer lingering and mellowing the approaching winter.

The faint, smoky haze of the atmosphere, the clear sky, the warm sun, the brilliant-hued vegetation in the woods, the faint cawing of crows in the distance, and the flight of birds overhead, looking like mathematical figures in India-ink gliding across the blue heavens, the delicious languor everywhere: all these were at their best, and he who was wandering through the rainbow-tinted forest, where the sleepy waters flowed, could well understand why it was the pioneers, like Daniel Boone, Simon Kenton, and others, turned their backs on civilization, and, plunging into the wilderness, buried themselves for months from the sight of their fellow-men.

Sam Harper was moving quietly toward the north, when it seemed to him that a large leaf suddenly blew forward from beneath his feet and was carried swiftly over the ground, straight ahead and away from him.

Looking closely, he discovered that it was a plump quail which he had startled, and which was speeding from him. Although the bird has short legs it runs very swiftly, and it was gone almost before Sam identified it.

"Ah, if I could only get a shot at you," said the lad, his mouth fairly watering, "what a splendid supper you would make!"

The words were yet in his mouth, when a sudden whirring sound broke the air, and he caught a glimpse of a second quail flying like an arrow below the principal limbs.

Sam raised his rifle as quick as a flash, took aim as best he could, and fired. Even the great Dr. Carver would have missed under such circumstances, and the lad came nowhere near hitting the game.

So swift was the flight of the bird, that as soon as the trigger was pulled and Sam looked for it it had vanished. That man who handles the rifle must be wonderfully skillful to bring down one of those birds on the wing.

It is curious how the name of the common quail is disputed and varied. There are plenty who will insist that I should have called this bird a partridge, when, in point of fact, there is no true representative of the partridge in America.

The spruce partridge is the Canada grouse; the partridge of New England is the ruffed grouse; the partridge of the Middle and Southern States is the quail, of which several varieties are called partridges; while in Europe the birds which are called quails are in reality partridges.

Without tiring my readers by attempting anything like a scientific discussion of the question, I may say there are a dozen species of quails found in North and Central America and the West Indies, and Mr. Baird proposes that, as neither the name quail, partridge, nor pheasant is properly given to any American bird, the species to which I refer should be called the Bob White.

If this should be done, the smallest urchin will be able to recognize the species from its peculiar call.

Sam Harper would have been glad indeed if he could have secured one of these delicious birds for supper, but there was little prospect of doing so. The game looks so much like the brown and mottled leaves among which it searches for food, that a hunter would almost place his foot upon one without observing it, while the nest of the quail or partridge is almost as impossible to find as the remains of an elephant in Ceylon, where it is said no such remains have ever been discovered.

One of the lessons Sam had learned from his father was to reload his gun immediately after firing it, so as to be ready for any emergency. Accordingly, before stirring from his place, he threw out the shell from his breech-loader and replaced it with a new cartridge.

Just as he did so, he heard the report of a gun only a short distance to the left, at a point where Herbert Watrous should have been.

"He's scared up something," was the natural conclusion of Sam, who smiled as he added; "I wonder whether he could hit a bear a dozen feet off with that wonderful Remington of his. It's a good weapon, and I wish I owned one; but I wouldn't start out to hunt big game until I learned something about it."

The boy waited a minute, listening for some signal from his companion, but none was heard and he moved on again.

Sam, like many an amateur hunter, began to appreciate the value of a trained hunting dog. Bowser was not a pure-blooded hound; he was fat and he was faultily trained. He had stumbled upon the trail of the buck by accident and had plunged ahead in pursuit, until "pumped," when he seemed to lose all interest in the sport.

He now stayed close to Sam, continually looking up in his face as if to ask him when he was going to stop the nonsense and go back home.

He scarcely pricked his ears when the quail ran ahead of him, and paid no attention to the whirring made by the other. He had had all he wanted of that kind of amusement and showed no disposition to tire himself any further.

CHAPTER XIX.

AN UNEXPECTED LESSON.

As it was the height of the hunting season, the reports of guns were heard at varying distances through the woods, so that Sam could only judge when they were fired by his friends from their nearness to him.

He was well satisfied that the last shot was from the Remington of Herbert, while the one that preceded it a few minutes, he was convinced came from the muzzle-loader of Nick Ribsam, owned by Mr. Marston.

"The boys seem to have found something too do, but I don't believe they have seen anything of the bear—hallo!"

His last exclamation was caused by his unexpected arrival at a clearing, in the center of which stood a log cabin, while the half acre surrounding it showed that it had been cultivated during the season to the highest extent.

There was that air of thrift and cleanliness about the place which told the lad that whoever lived within was industrious, frugal, and neat.

"That's a queer place to build a house," said Sam, as he surveyed the scene; "no one can earn a living there, and it must make a long walk to reach the neighborhood where work is to be had."

Prompted by a natural curiosity, Sam walked over the faintly marked path until he stepped upon the piece of hewed log, which answered for a porch, directly in front of the door.

Although the latch string hung invitingly out, he did not pull it, but knocked rather gently.

"Come in!" was called out in a female voice, and the boy immediately opened the door.

A pleasing, neatly-clad young woman was working with her dishes at a table, while a fat chub of a boy, about two years old, was playing on the floor with a couple of kittens.

The mother, as she evidently was, turned her head so as to face the visitor, nodded cheerily, bade him good afternoon, and told him to help himself to one of the chairs, whose bottoms were made of white mountain ash, as fine and pliable as silken ribbons.

Sam was naturally courteous, and, thanking the lady for her invitation, he sat down, placing his cap on his knee. He said he was out on a hunt with some friends, and coming upon the cabin thought he would make a call, and learn whether he could be of any service to the lady and her child.

The mother thanked him, and said that fortunately she was not in need of any help, as her husband was well and able to provide her with all she needed.

Without giving the conversation in detail, it may be said that Sam Harper learned a lesson, during his brief stay in that humble cabin, which will go with him through life: it was a lesson of cheerfulness and contentment, to which he often refers, and which makes him thankful that he was led to turn aside from his sport even for a short while.

The husband of the woman worked for a farmer who lived fully four miles away, on the northern edge of the woods, and who paid only scant wages. The employee walked the four miles out so as to reach the farm by seven o'clock in the morning, and he did not leave until six in the evening. He did this summer and winter, through storm and sunshine, and was happy.

He lived in the lonely log cabin, because his employer owned it and gave him the rent free. It had been erected by some wood-choppers several years before, and was left by them when through with their contract, so that it was nothing to any one who did not occupy it.

The young man, although now the embodiment of rugged health and strength, had lain on a bed of sickness for six months, during which he hovered between life and death. His wife never left his side during that time for more than a few minutes, and the physician was scarcely less faithful. At last the wasting fever vanished, and the husband and father came back to health and strength again.

But he was in debt to the extent of $200, and he and his wife determined on the most rigid economy until the last penny should be paid.

"If Fred keeps his health," said the cheery woman, "we shall be out of debt at the end of two years more. Won't you bring your friends and stay with us to-night?"

This invitation was given with great cordiality, and Sam would have been glad to accept it, but he declined, through consideration for the brave couple, who would certainly be put to inconvenience by entertaining three visitors.

Sam thanked her for her kindness, and, rising to go, drew back the door and remarked:

"I notice you have a good rifle over the mantle; I don't see how your husband can get much time to use it."

"He doesn't; it is I who shoot the game, which saves half the cost of food; but," added the plucky little woman, "there is one game which I am very anxious to bring down."

"What is that?"

"*A bear.*"

"Do you know whether there are any in the woods?"

"There is one, and I think more. My husband has seen it twice, and he took the gun with him when going to work, in the hope of gaining a chance to shoot it; but, when I caught sight of it on the edge of the clearing, he thought it best to leave the rifle for me to use."

"Why are you so anxious to shoot the bear?" asked Sam.

"Well, it isn't a very pleasant neighbor, and I have to keep little Tommy in the house all the time for fear the brute will seize him. Then, beside that, the bear has carried off some of Mr. Bailey's (that's the man my husband works for) pigs, and has so frightened his family that Mr. Bailey said he would give us twenty dollars for the hide of every bear we brought him."

"I hope it may be your fortune to shoot all in the woods," said Sam, as he bade her good-day again, and passed out and across the clearing into the forest.

"That's about the bravest woman I ever saw," said the lad to himself, as he moved thoughtfully in the direction of the limestone-rock, where it was agreed the three should meet to spend the night; "she ought to win, and if this crowd of bear hunters succeed in bagging the old fellow we will present him to her."

The thought was a pleasing one to Sam, who walked a short way farther, when he added, with a grim smile, "But I don't think that bear will lose any night's sleep on account of being disturbed by *this* crowd."

CHAPTER XX.

BOWSER PROVES HIMSELF OF SOME USE.

Sam Harper saw, from the position of the sun in the heavens, that he had stayed longer than he intended to in the cabin, and the short afternoon was drawing to a close.

He therefore moved at a brisk walk for a quarter of a mile, Bowser trotting at his heels as though he thought such a laborious gait uncalled for; but, as the lad then observed that the large limestone was not far away, he slackened his pace, and sat down on a fallen tree to rest.

"This is a queer sort of a hunt," he said to himself, "and I don't see what chance there is of any one of us three doing anything at all. Bowser isn't worth a copper to hunt with; all there was in him expended itself when he chased the buck and let it get away from him—hallo, Bowser, what's the matter with you?"

The hound just then began acting as though he felt the slighting remarks of his master, and meant to make him sorry therefor.

He uttered several sharp yelps and began circling around the fallen tree on which Sam was sitting. He went with what might be called a nervous gallop, frequently turning about and circumnavigating the lad and the log in the opposite direction.

All the time he kept up his barking and demonstrations, now and then running up to Sam, galloping several paces away, and then looking toward him and barking again with great vigor.

Sam watched his antics with amusement and interest.

"He acts as though he wanted me to follow him from this spot, though I cannot understand why he wants me to do that, since he is so lazy he would be glad to lie down and stay here till morning."

Studying the maneuvers of the hound, Sam became satisfied that the brute was seeking to draw him away from the fallen tree on which he was sitting.

The dog became more excited every minute. He trotted back and forth, running up to his young master and then darting off again, looking appealingly toward Sam, who finally saw that his actions meant something serious.

"I don't know why he wishes me to leave, but he has some reason for it, and I will try to find out."

Sam slowly rose from the fallen oak tree on which he was sitting, and as he did so his cap fairly lifted from his head with terror.

He caught the glint and scintillation in the sunlight of something on the ground on the other side of the trunk, and separated from him only by the breadth thereof, at the same instant that his ear detected the whirring rattle which told the fact that an immense rattlesnake had coiled itself therefor, and had just given its warning signal that it meant to strike.

Sam Harper never made such a quick leap in all his life as he did, when he bounded several feet from the log, with a yell as if the ground beneath him had become suddenly red-hot.

There is nothing on the broad earth which is held in such universal abhorrence as a snake, the sight of which sends a shiver of disgust and dread over nearly every one that looks upon it.

When Sam sat down on the fallen tree, he was probably almost near enough for the coiled *crotalus* to bury its fangs in him. It reared its head, and, without uttering its customary warning, most likely measured the intervening space with the purpose of striking.

The instinct of Bowser at this juncture told him of the peril of his master, and he began his demonstrations, intended to draw him away from the spot. At the same time, his barking, and trotting back and forth, diverted the attention of the rattlesnake to the hound, and thereby prevented him striking the unsuspicious boy.

It must have been, also, that during these few minutes the serpent vibrated his tail more than once, for the nature of the reptile leads him to do so; but the sound could not have been very loud, as it failed to attract the attention of Sam until he rose from the log and turned partly about.

The boy moved around the head of the fallen tree, so as to place himself on the same side with the rattlesnake, and then he spent a minute or two in contemplating him at that safe distance.

He was a large one, with sixteen rattles and a button. He lay coiled in several perfect rings, with his tail softly vibrating and his head thrown back, as if he expected his enemy to come nigh enough for him to bury his curved needle-like fangs in some portion of his body, injecting his poison, so deadly that nothing could have saved the boy from dying within a few minutes.

The first natural feeling which comes over one when he sees a crawling snake is to kill it, and Sam Harper did not wait long before yielding to his inclination.

Standing less than a rod distant, he brought his gun to his shoulder, and sighted at the head of the venomous reptile, which was held almost stationary, while the crimson tongue darted in and out as if it were a tiny spray of blood.

The aim was true, and the head was shattered as though the cartridge had exploded within it. The body made a few furious writhings and struggles, and then became still.

Sam viewed the ruin he had wrought for a minute or so, and then, appreciating the service his dog had wrought him, he turned and patted the animal.

"You're a fine dog, Bowser, and I forgive you for being good for nothing."

CHAPTER XXI.

FACE TO FACE.

Herbert Watrous, when he separated from his companions on that balmy afternoon in Indian summer, assumed a loftiness of bearing which was far from genuine.

The fact was, he felt dissatisfied with himself, or rather with the rifle which his indulgent father had presented to him only a few weeks before.

"I don't like the way the thing behaves," he said, as he stopped to examine it; "father paid one hundred and twenty-five dollars for it, and it was warranted the best. It's pretty hard to hit a deer a quarter of a mile off, but I ought to have brought down that squirrel which was only a hundred feet distant."

He turned the weapon over and over in his hand, looked down the barrel, tried the hammer and trigger, carefully examined the wind-gauge and vernier rear-sights, but could not see that anything was out of order.

"I'm afraid it was my fault," he said, with a sigh, "but it will never do to let the boys know it. I'll insist that I struck the buck, though I'm afraid I didn't."

After going a little ways he noticed he was walking over a path which was not marked very distinctly; it was, in fact, the route which Mr. Fred Fowler, the industrious dweller in the log cabin, had worn for himself in going to and from his work.

"That's lucky," said the lad, "for it's much easier traveling over a path like that than tramping among the trees, where you have to walk twice as far as there is any need of—confound it!"

This impatient remark was caused by a protruding branch, which just then caught Herbert under the chin and almost lifted him off his feet.

The boy was sensible enough to understand that his failure to display any good marksmanship was due to his own want of practice rather than to any fault of his piece.

"That Nick Ribsam can beat me out of my boots; I never heard of such a thing as 'barking' a squirrel till he showed me how it is done, and he used a gun that is older than himself. Well, Nick was always smarter than other boys; he is younger than I, and I have taken sparring lessons of the best teachers in the country, while he never heard of such a thing as science in using his fists; but he just sailed into me that day, and the first thing I knew he had me down, and was banging himself on me so hard that I have never got over the flattening out—hallo!"

A gray squirrel, flirting its bushy tail, whisked across the path in front of him that moment, scampered up a hickory and perched itself near the top, where it offered the best chance for a shot that one could wish.

"Now I'll see what I can do," muttered Herbert, sighting at the saucy little fellow, who seemed to be ridiculing his purpose of reaching it with a bullet at such a height.

The young hunter aimed with great care, pressed the trigger, and, as the sharp report rang through the woods, the squirrel came tumbling to the ground, with its skull shattered.

Herbert Watrous was surprised and delighted, scarcely believing in his own success. He picked up the slain rodent and saw that its destruction had been caused by the bullet he fired.

"That's business," he exclaimed, with a thrill of pride; "but why couldn't I shoot that way when Nick and Sam were looking at me? I know how the thing is done now, and when we get together I'll give them some lessons in marksmanship."

He left the squirrel on the ground, but had not gone far when a new idea struck him and he came back, picked it up, and put it in his game-bag.

"If I show them a squirrel, they can't help believing that I shot him."

The serious question which Herbert had been discussing with himself, ever since being alone, was what he would do if he should happen to come upon the bear. He had not quite so much confidence in his gun as he had when he started out, though the shooting of the squirrel brought back considerable of his natural assurance.

The conclusion he reached was that it would be just as well if he and bruin did not meet. Excellent as was his Remington, it was not a repeating rifle, and he was afraid that one shot, even if well aimed, would not be enough.

"If I had a Henry, which shoots sixteen shots in sixteen seconds, I could fill him so full of lead that he couldn't run fast enough to overtake me if I didn't happen to kill him."

But the Henry, which he desired so much, was beyond his reach, and it was idle to wish for it.

Accordingly, he slung his gun over his shoulder in true sportsman style, and strode along the path until the greater part of the distance was passed, when, like his friends, he found a fallen tree at a convenient spot and sat down for a rest.

Herbert, in his luxurious home in the city, had become accustomed to irregular hours, so that it was now the most natural thing in the world for him to fall asleep and not open his eyes until he shivered with cold and it was growing dark around him.

He started up in no little surprise, and, recalling where he was, hastened along the path toward the camp.

"They'll be worried almost to death about me," was his thought, "and I shouldn't wonder if they start out to hunt me up. Ah!"

The reverberating report of a rifle came from the direction of the limestone rock, and he felt no doubt that it was meant as a signal to direct him.

Herbert replied by firing his own gun in the air and shouting that he was coming. He did not forget to place another cartridge in his rifle, for, truth to tell, he was a little nervous over this lonely tramp through the woods at such a late hour.

He listened, and heard the answering shout of Sam Harper, and, communication being thus established, Herbert held his peace and hastened forward as best he could in the faint moonlight.

"I hope I won't meet any sort of game now," was the wish of the lad, "for I am in a hurry to join the boys—"

Could he believe his eyes!

He had hardly given expression to the wish, when a dark mass loomed up to sight directly ahead of him, and he plainly saw the gleam and glow of a pair of frightful eyes fixed upon him. He was sure, too, that he had heard the threatening growl of the monster, which might well believe he had the youngster in his power.

"It's the bear, as sure as I'm alive!" gasped Herbert. "There's no getting away from him! Heaven save me from missing, for if my gun fails me now, it is all over! He won't give me time to climb a tree, and I *must* shoot!"

CHAPTER XXII.

THE "VACANT CHAIR."

It is hard to imagine a more trying situation than that of Master Herbert

Watrous, who, while walking along a path in the woods, saw by the faint moonlight what he believed to be the figure of an enormous black bear, sitting on its haunches, and waiting for him to move either forward or backward before springing upon him.

He shuddered with fear, but, with a courage hardly to be expected in his case, he drew up his rifle, sighted as best he could, and fired point-blank at the brute, when no more than a rod separated the two.

It was impossible to miss, even with such an unsteady aim, and the lad had not a particle of doubt that he had hit him; but had he inflicted a mortal wound?

Without waiting an unnecessary second, Herbert flung out the shell of the cartridge and placed a new one in the breech. His hands trembled so that he could hardly keep from dropping it, but he succeeded better than would have been supposed.

Once more the gun was raised, and the leaden missile was buried in the dark object.

But it did not stir, and the amazed lad was transfixed. What did it mean?

"I'll give him another, and if that don't answer—"

From out the gloom in front he discerned a figure advancing upon him, but a second glance showed that it was a man instead of a wild animal.

"Hallo, my friend? what are you firing at?"

The voice was such a cheery one that the courage of Herbert instantly came back, and it may be said that he was never gladder in all his life to see a person.

"Why, I thought that was a wild animal—that is, a bear, in the path in front of me; what is it?"

The man laughed heartily.

"The path makes a little bend right there, so it is not in, but beside the path; it is an oak stump on which you have been wasting your lead."

"But those glaring eyes—"

"That is fox-fire, which does look odd in the night-time."

"But I heard it growling."

"Be assured it was all imagination, my young friend; there is no bear or wild animal near us—at least he hasn't shown himself yet."

"Well, I'm blamed glad to hear it, for there isn't much fun in hunting wild beasts when it is too dark to aim well: may I ask how it is you happen along here without a gun?"

"I live only a little ways off, and, if you will go back with me, I will be glad to entertain you over night."

"I'm obliged to you, but I have two friends who are expecting me, up by the rock yonder."

"I judged you belonged to the party, but there is only one of them there, unless the other has come since I left. The one named Harper, who called at my house this afternoon, is there, and has started his camp fire. He is impatient for the others to come in, and asked me to tell you, if we met, that he particularly wished you to 'hurry up your cakes'—I suppose you know what that means."

"I do, and will bid you good-night."

They exchanged pleasant greetings, and separated, each to pursue his own way.

Herbert was anxious to join his friends; for the fact that he had fired into a stump, under the belief that it was a bear, was no proof that the dreaded quadruped was not somewhere in the neighborhood.

As the path, which he was able to keep without difficulty, led by the rock where the three lads were to meet, he had not gone far when he caught the starlike twinkle of a point of light, which told him he was not far from camp.

"Hallo, Sam, are you there?" called out Herbert, while yet a considerable distance off.

"Yes. What makes you so late?" was the impatient response and question.

Without pausing to reply, Herbert hurried forward and a few minutes later joined Sam Harper, who had a large fire going, and had broiled a squirrel and a rabbit, both of which were in fine condition.

"Where's Nick?" asked Sam, as soon as he saw the youth was alone.

"How should I know anything about him? I haven't seen him since we parted."

"It's mighty queer, any way you may look at it; Nick is always the most prompt to keep any bargain he made, and I haven't seen anything of him for hours. He ought to have been here the very first."

"Have you signaled to him?"

"I have fired off my gun, and shouted and whistled till my cheeks ache, and I haven't had the first show of an answer."

The manner in which these disheartening words were uttered showed that Sam Harper was ill at ease, not so much over the continued absence of Nick, as from his utter silence. It was fully understood by all, that, if anything happened to either one, he was to signal immediately to the others.

Neither Herbert nor Sam had heard Nick's rifle, though it might have been discharged without recognition by them.

Herbert had been asleep so long that he could have missed the report very readily, while Sam was so far from Nick that the sound of his gun could have been mistaken for that fired by some wandering hunter, unknown to either.

Every few minutes, Sam halloed or whistled, after Nick's favorite manner of signaling, and then the two bent their heads and listened for the answer, which came not.

The broiled game remained untasted, for Sam's appetite was suspended, and Herbert refused to eat while his companion was in such mental trouble.

"There's no use of talking," finally exclaimed Sam, unable to repress his uneasiness, "something has gone wrong with Nick, and I'm bound to find out what it is."

CHAPTER XXIII.

HUNTING A BUCK.

It will be remembered that when Nick Ribsam left his companions, early in the afternoon, it was with the resolution to find out whether the showy shot made by Herbert Watrous at the buck, had done the execution he claimed for it.

This forced him to make a much longer detour than did Sam Harper, and, as he was obliged to move with great caution, he found no time to sit down and rest or sleep.

The more he reflected on the exploit which Herbert attempted, the more did he doubt it.

"I suppose they hit a target a mile off, as Sam told me; but that is when they know the exact distance. No person can hit a deer a quarter of a mile away, unless he does it by chance. Herbert proved he can't shoot anything close to him, and it isn't likely he hit the deer by accident, for such accidents don't happen unless it's a person that you don't want to hurt."

But he had started out to find the truth of the matter, and it was in accordance with his disposition to do so, if it was possible.

Nick knew that if the buck which they had seen was anywhere in the neighborhood, it was necessary to proceed with extreme caution to avoid giving alarm. The wonder was that it had shown itself after the fright caused by the dog.

The drowsy autumn afternoon was well advanced when the boy saw, from his surroundings, that he was close to the spot where the deer stood when Herbert fired at it with his long-range rifle. There was the rock, but the animal was invisible.

Just beyond was an oak which had been upturned by some wrenching tornado or storm. The roots protruded upward and from the sides, the dirt still clinging to them, so that the bottom spread out like a fan.

The base of the trunk lay flat on the ground, but the branching limbs supported the top to that extent that it was raised five or six feet from the earth. Consequently, it sloped away in an incline from the crested summit to the base.

Such a sight is not unusual in any forest, for it is the general fashion of trees to fall that way; but Nick was struck by the evident fact that, although the oak was uprooted, as it is termed, yet enough connection with the ground remained to afford nourishment, and to keep life within it.

He started toward it, but had moved only a few steps when a slight rustling in the undergrowth arrested his attention. Stopping short he looked about him, and, with an amazement which can hardly be imagined, saw the buck within fifty feet of him.

He was in a clump of undergrowth, and was browsing on some tender shoots. His position was such that his side was toward Nick, who first caught sight of his antlers above the bushes: and it was a remarkable thing that he did not detect the approach of the young hunter, despite the caution he used.

The sight was so unexpected that Nick was taken aback, and had a spasm of that nervous affection which sometimes seizes the inexperienced hunter, and is known as "buck fever."

Knowing that the game would bound away with the speed of the wind the instant he scented danger, the lad brought up his rifle and pointed at him.

Poor Nick shook as if he had a chill; it was impossible to control his nerves; but, aiming as best he could, he fired. The deer was "hit hard," though not so hard as young Ribsam meant and most ardently desired.

Dropping the breech of his gun, Nick looked to see the result of his shot, and found it amazing to a startling degree.

The buck, which was a noble fellow, stopped browsing, and, with his head thrown high in air, looked around to learn where his assailant was. Catching sight of the staring lad, the animal emitted a furious sniff and charged upon him at full speed.

This is a most unusual thing for a deer to do, though many a hunter has been killed by a wounded buck or moose, who has turned upon and attacked him with the fury of a tiger.

"He turned on his heel and ran with might and main for the fallen tree."

Nick Ribsam thought it very singular, but he thought it very alarming as well, and, without waiting to watch matters further, he turned on his heel and ran with might and main for the fallen tree.

The lusty youngster was a good runner, but the buck made three times as much speed as he "went for him," with head lowered like a charging bull.

Nick had to think fast, but fast as he thought he couldn't see how the fallen oak was to offer him refuge against the fury of the animal, and, unless it did so, he was in a bad predicament.

It was impossible to reach any tree in time to climb out of reach, as Nellie did when pursued by the bear, and the highest portion of the prostrate trunk would not protect him from the antlers of the savage buck.

There was no use for the empty rifle as it seemed, and Nick was on the point of throwing it away, when it occurred to him that it might still serve as a weapon of defense.

"I will club it and see what can be done."

CHAPTER XXIV.

HUNTED BY A BUCK.

Glancing over his shoulder, Nick Ribsam kept informed of the movements of his fierce foe, who was certainly carrying things with a hurricane rush.

Finding there was no getting away from him, Nick, just as he reached the fallen tree, whirled around and, grasping his rifle by the barrel, swung the stock back over his shoulder and poised himself for the blow, which he believed must decide his own fate.

The boy made a formidable-looking picture; but it was all lost on the buck, which did not halt nor slacken his pace.

It was a terrifying sight as he plunged toward the lad with lowered head and glowering front, for the deer was an exceptionally large and powerful one, and he meant to kill the individual that had sent the bullet into his side, and from which the red blood was already streaming.

It may be said just here, that Nick Ribsam no longer doubted the failure of the long-range shot of Herbert Watrous.

The imperiled lad drew a deep respiration, poised himself on his advanced foot, and, swinging to one side, with a view of avoiding the full force of the charge, he brought down the stock of his gun with the utmost strength he could command.

It descended with great power—so far as a ten-year-old boy is concerned—but it was not sufficient to throw the buck off his base nor to interfere with his plan of procedure.

He struck the lad with tremendous force, sending the gun flying from his grasp and knocking Nick fully a dozen feet. Never in all his life had the boy received such a terrific shock, which drove the breath from his body and sent him spinning, as it seemed, through twenty yards of space.

Poor Nick believed half his bones were broken and that he was mortally hurt; but the result of the charge was most extraordinary.

As the antlers of the buck struck him he was thrown like a limp dummy toward the fallen tree, and, in reality, his greatest peril was therefrom. Had he been driven with full momentum against the solid trunk, he would have been killed as if smitten by a lightning stroke.

But his feet were entangled in some way and he fell headlong, his forehead within a few inches of the bark, and his head itself was driven under the trunk, which at that point was perhaps a foot above the ground.

Instinctively the nearly senseless lad did the only thing that could save him. He crawled under the trunk, so that it stood like a roof over him.

His head was toward the base, and he pushed along until the lessening space would not permit him to go further.

Thus he lay parallel with the uprooted tree, his feet at a point where the bark almost touched his heels, the space growing less and less toward his shoulders, until the back of his head rested against the shaggy bark and his nose touched the leaves.

He had scarcely done this when he heard a thud at his elbow: it was made by the knife-like hoofs of the buck, who, rearing on his hind legs, gathered his two front ones close together and brought them down with such force that, had they fallen on the body of the lad, as was intended, they would have cut into him like the edge of a powerfully driven ax.

As it was, the shielding tree trunk prevented it, and, grazing the bark, they were driven into the yielding earth half a foot deep.

The buck immediately reared and repeated the terrible blow several times, missing the body of the lad by what may be called a hair's breadth.

The animal was in a fury, and, believing his foe was at his mercy, he showed him none.

Nick heard the first thump of the sharp hoofs as they cut their way into the earth, and then his head seemed to spin, as though he had been whirled around with inconceivable velocity; innumerable stars danced before his eyes, he felt as if shooting through space, and then consciousness left him.

The buck could know nothing of this, and, had he known it, his actions would not have been affected. He continued his rearing and plunging until he saw he was inflicting no injury. Then he stopped, backed off several paces, and, lowering his head, tried to dislodge the lad from his place of refuge.

But the breadth of his antlers prevented success, which would have placed Nick just where he could finish him. The oak barred his progress, stopping the head and horns when they were almost against the body.

Then the buck reared and struck again, trying all manner of maneuvers which his instinct suggested, but providentially none of them succeeded.

All this time Nick Ribsam, who had been so badly bruised, was oblivious of the efforts against his life. Had he possessed his faculties, he could not have done anything more for his protection than he did, by lying motionless, extended along and below the trunk of the oak.

But the lusty, rugged nature of the lad soon asserted itself, and he began rallying from the shock. A reaction gradually set in, and slowly his senses returned.

It was a considerable time, however, before he realized where he was and what had befallen him. His head was still ringing, as though the clangor of a hundred anvils were sounding in his ears, and, when he drew a deep breath, a pain, as if made by a knife, was in his side.

He listened, but heard nothing of his enemy. Then, with a great labor and more suffering, he pushed himself a few inches backward, so as to give some freedom to his body and to enable him to move his head.

Turning his face, he peered out on his right: the buck was not visible in that direction.

Then he did the same toward the left: his enemy was invisible on that side also.

"He is gone," said the lad to himself, still afraid to venture from the shielding trunk that had been the means of saving him from the fury of the enraged deer.

Nick believed he was close at hand, waiting for him to make a move that would give another chance to assault him.

After several more minutes, the lad hitched farther backward, so that he was able to raise his head a few inches. This extended his field of observation, and, with a feeling of inexpressible relief, he still failed to catch sight of the game.

"I guess he got discouraged and left," said Nick, startled at the evidences of the buck's wrath so near him.

Finally the lad backed clear out from under the tree, and climbed to his feet; it was climbing in every sense, for he nearly cried with pain several times, and, still fearful that he had been seriously injured, he examined himself as best he could.

A few minutes convinced him that none of his bones was broken, although he afterward declared that he suspected his head had been fractured.

He now looked about for his gun and found it within a short distance, much scratched by the hard treatment it had received, but without any real injury.

Throwing the weapon over his shoulder, he started in the direction of the appointed rendezvous, and, as he did so, observed that it was already grown dark in the woods. Night had come, and he had quite a long distance to walk.

CHAPTER XXV.

THE CAMP FIRE.

But Nick Ribsam was full of grit, and, though every step he took caused him pain, he persevered with that grim resolution that was a part of his nature from his very birth.

After walking some distance he found the soreness and stiffness leaving him, and he straightened up with something of his natural vim and elasticity of spirits.

"There's one thing certain," he added, recalling his encounter with the buck, "I didn't have any one to help me out of that scrape, except the One who always helps him that helps himself; but I never wanted a friend more than then, and, if it hadn't been for that oak, it would have been the last of Nicholas Ribsam."

"There is another thing I have learned," he added, with that glimmer of humor which was sure to show itself, "I know considerable more than I did yesterday; I have a good idea of how it feels when a wounded buck *raises* you, and, after this, I won't shoot one of the creatures unless I'm sure of making a better shot than I did a while ago—hallo!"

Well might he utter the last exclamation, for at that moment he came upon the dead body of the buck, lying as he had fallen on the earth, when at last he succumbed to the wound received at the hands of Nick himself.

The boy stopped to examine it, for he was much impressed by the discovery.

"That came very near ending in the death of us both: nothing but the oak saved me. I wonder whether I am going right."

He raised his head from his examination, and looked about him, but he was without the means of judging whether he was following the proper direction or not. When leaving the scene of his encounter with the deer, he had taken the course that seemed to be right, without pausing until he could make himself certain in the matter.

This is pretty sure, in a majority of cases, to lead one astray, but it so happened with Nick that he headed in a bee-line for the camp, where the impatient Sam Harper was awaiting him.

But the error came afterward: he toiled forward without any guide, and soon began to turn to the left, so that he was in reality moving on the circumference of a large circle, without suspecting how much he wandered from the true course.

This peculiar mistake is made by many who are lost in the wilderness, and is supposed to be due to the fact that everybody is either right or left handed, instead of being ambidextrous as we all ought to be.

One side of the body being stronger than the other, we unconsciously exert the limb on that side the most, and swerve from a straight line, unless we have something to direct in the shape of a landmark or guiding-post.

It was not until Nick had gone a long ways out of the right course that he suspected his error: the appearance of the camp fire which Sam Harper had kindled, was what led him to stop and make the best investigation he could.

There was little else he could appeal to, and he was in doubt as to whether that had not been kindled by some other party; but fortunately, while he was debating the matter, he caught the faint but distinct signal of his friend, who was on the point of starting out to look for him.

Nick replied, and in the course of half an hour had joined Sam and Herbert by the fire.

They were relieved beyond expression to see the figure of the sturdy little fellow, as he emerged from the gloom, and took his seat around the camp fire.

They noticed that he limped, and knew something unusual must have taken place to delay him. He had the most attentive of listeners when he related his dangerous encounter with the buck, which came so nigh ending his life.

But, happily, he had come out without any serious injury, and the lads attacked their supper with the keenest of appetites.

"The reason the buck did not kill you," said Herbert, "was because he was disabled by the wound I gave him."

"He was struck by one bullet only, and that one was mine," said Nick, who saw no sense in deferring to the absurd claims of the youth.

"Possibly not, but we shall have to examine his carcass to make sure of that."

"I don't believe we shall have much time to look after dead deer," said Sam, "for I believe we are in the neighborhood of the very bear we're looking for."

His friends turned toward him for an explanation of this remark, which was uttered with all seriousness.

"Bowser has been acting very queer for the last half-hour."

"I think he has acted queer all day," observed Nick.

"I did not consider him of much account until he saved me from the rattlesnake this afternoon; after that, I'm ready to believe he's got a good deal more sense than you are willing to think."

Then Sam told his story, and added that the hound had left the vicinity of the fire several times, and, going some distance in the woods, had come back, giving utterance to a peculiar whine. At the same time he looked up in the face of his master with much the same expression as he did when seeking to warn him of his danger from the poisonous serpent.

"There he goes now!" suddenly exclaimed Sam; "just watch him!"

Bowser had been stretched out near enough to the fire to receive much of its warmth, and appeared to be asleep. All at once he threw up his head and sniffed the air, as though he scented something; then he rose, with a low whine, and trotted straight out in the gloom.

The lads listened attentively for some sound from him, but all remained still. At the end of ten minutes he came trotting to view again, and walked straight up to his master, looked up in his face, wagging his tail, and whined again.

"You can depend on it," said Sam, "he has made some discovery, though I have no idea what it is."

"Let's follow him and find out."

It was Nick Ribsam who made the proposal; the others were inclined to hold back, but the plucky little fellow insisted, and it was agreed that Bowser's secret should be learned by keeping him company to the spot which he visited.

CHAPTER XXVI.

AN UNEXPECTED ATTACK.

The three boys had scarcely agreed to the proposition to follow the hound, when Bowser, as if he understood their intention, rose from the ground where he had been lying, close to the camp fire, looked sharply out in the gloom of the surrounding woods, and then moved along the same course he had taken several times before.

He did not trot, but walked with a deliberate gait, as if he felt the importance of being the leader of such a party.

"It must be a wild animal," said Sam, in an undertone, "or Bowser wouldn't act that way."

"It's the bear, of course; see that your guns are ready, and when you fire be sure you don't miss," warned Herbert.

An idea suddenly occurred to Nick Ribsam.

"All wild animals are afraid of fire: let's each take a torch to keep him off."

The others eagerly caught up a blazing brand and strode forward with more confidence than ever.

Herbert Watrous, who was sensible that he had not made such an exhibition before the others as he desired, placed himself at the head of the little company.

He hardly would have done this, had he not been certain that the flaming brands would act as a shield to keep away the wild animal, whatever its nature.

Each lad found it a little awkward to carry his loaded and cocked rifle in one hand and the flaming stick of wood in the other. It cannot be said there was any special difficulty in the task itself, but if a crisis came the boy would have to surrender one of his weapons.

The young hunters formed a picturesque group as they moved forward in Indian file, each holding a burning torch above his head and swinging it so as to keep the blaze going, while his gun was trailed in the other hand.

The hound Bowser was at the head, Herbert Watrous next, Sam Harper followed, and Nick Ribsam, who still limped slightly, brought up the rear.

The hound showed an intelligence which would have been surprising but for his action respecting the rattlesnake. He kept on a slow walk, so as not to leave his friends, and now and then looked at them, as if to make sure they were not trying to shrink from an important duty.

"Keep your torches going," called out Herbert, in a husky whisper, as he swung his own so vigorously that a large piece dropped off, and, falling on his foot, caused him to leap up with an exclamation of affright.

The fact was, they had gone no more than a hundred feet from the camp fire when Herbert began to feel that he had not shown enough care in picking out his torch, for the blaze was feeble, and, in spite of continued nursing, showed a tendency to collapse altogether.

"Keep close to me, boys," he said, waiting for Sam to come still nearer, "for I don't like the way this torch is behaving; I believe it is going out altogether, and I think I'll get a better—"

"*Look out! there he is now!*" exclaimed Sam, in no little excitement.

As he uttered the warning words, Bowser turned squarely about and ran back to where his master had halted with the smoking torch, and crouched at his feet, whining and appealing for protection against some enemy.

Just then a savage sniff was heard, followed instantly by the sound of hoofs, as the unknown animal charged upon Herbert Watrous, who was whirling his half-expired torch around his head with such swiftness that it made a ring of fire, similar to those which all boys delight to look upon during the pyrotechnic displays on the Fourth of July.

Herbert was so impressed with the importance of this action, that he threw all his energy in it, stooping down and rising on his tip-toes with the motion of the torch, and grunting hard and with much regularity, as he always did when exerting himself with unusual vigor.

He caught the warning cry of Sam and the rattle of the hoofs at the same instant.

"*Shoot him! Shoot him!*" he shouted to his friends, who could not gain the view of the beast necessary to make the shot safe for Herbert himself.

The savage creature, from some reason, probably because the torch was less formidable, made for the city youth, who was not aware of his danger until too late.

The brute went directly between his outspread feet, and, lifting him on his back, carried him several paces, when Herbert, his gun, torch, and himself, mixed up in great confusion, rolled off backward, turning a partial somersault and landing solidly on his head, his gun going off in the confusion and adding to it.

Sam Harper threw down his torch, so as to use his rifle, but he saw Herbert's dilemma and waited the chance to shoot without danger of harming him; but the partial extinguishment of his own torch, and the total blotting out of Herbert's, rendered the risk still greater.

While he stood, with gun partly raised and hand on the trigger, Herbert rolled off, but Sam had not time to catch the fact when the beast shot between his legs, and he felt himself lifted off his feet and fairly whizzing through the air.

Nick Ribsam's torch was burning brightly and illuminated the whole scene. He was in a stooping position, holding his flaming brand so he could see everything, and he was laughing so hard that he could hardly keep from falling to the ground from weakness.

He had recognized the animal, which they had held in such terror, as a large hog that had doubtless wandered in the woods so long with his mates, eating the acorns and nuts fallen from the trees, that he was half wild and ready to attack any one who came near him.

The hog was a lank, bony fellow, with great strength and swiftness of gait, and, like his fiercer brother the wild boar of Europe, he possessed undoubted courage.

"Well, if that ain't the funniest sight I ever saw!" roared Nick, bending himself almost double with laughter; "we thought it was a bear, and I guess Herbert and Sam are sure it is a royal Bengal tiger or mad elephant—"

CHAPTER XXVII.

WAS IT A JOKE?

At that instant, Nick Ribsam felt himself suddenly lifted in air and spinning forward with great speed on the back of the vigorous hog, which plunged between his rather short legs.

The astounded lad instantly stopped laughing, and, dropping his gun and torch, grasped at something to sustain himself against the peril, the nature of which he could hardly guess.

The hog had struck him from the front, so that Nick was seated in reverse position on his back. The object which he grasped was the spiral tail of the animal, but, before he could make his grip certain, the porker swerved so suddenly to one side that Nick rolled off and bumped against a tree.

His body was not hurt to one half the extent that his feelings were, for he heard Sam Harper roaring with mirth, loud enough to be heard half a mile; and as Nick hastily clambered upon his feet, he was certain Herbert's cracked laugh was also rending the night air.

The porker, having made the round and paid his tribute to each member of the company in turn, whisked off into the woods, with a triumphant grunt, as if to say, "I guess you folks and your dog will let me alone now."

As soon as the boys found their guns, and restored two of the torches to a blaze, they looked at each other and gave way to their unrestrained mirth for several minutes before they could speak so as to be understood.

Never had a pompous expedition ended more ignobly: they had started out to attack a fierce black bear, and unexpectedly were overturned by a large-sized pig, which resented the interference with his slumber.

Some naturalists maintain that many animals possess a sense of the humorous, and it looked as though the sluggish Bowser enjoyed the joke as much as did the victims; for, when the latter made their way back to the camp fire, they saw the hound stretched out close to the warm blaze with his head between his paws and apparently asleep; but, watching him closely, he was seen to open one of his eyes, just a little ways, and, surveying them a minute, he closed it to open again a minute later.

No animal could have said more plainly:

"I've got the joke on you this time, boys, and I'm laughing so hard that I can't keep my eyes open."

"I tell you there is a good deal more in the heads of brutes than many of us think," said Nick Ribsam, after he had studied the actions of the hound; "I believe he wanted to make us believe there was some sort of game out there so as to play the fool with us."

"Do you think he foresaw the trick of the hog?" asked Herbert, who was rubbing his bruised elbows and knees.

"That would have been impossible, for we could not have foreseen it ourselves if we had arranged the joke; he simply meant to mislead us, and then we acted the fool for *his* amusement."

It looked very much as if Nick Ribsam was correct in his supposition, and that Bowser enjoyed even more than they the shrewd trick he had played on them.

"I suppose there are several hundred hogs wandering through the woods," said Nick, "picking up acorns and nuts that have fallen off the trees, and making a good living at it."

"Yes, lots of them have been running wild for weeks and months," added Sam, "and when their owners try to gather them in, there will be trouble, for it doesn't take hogs long to become savage."

"It didn't take that hog very long, I'm sure," observed Herbert, sitting down with care upon the ground.

"But how was it there was but *one*?" asked Sam.

"There wasn't need of any more than one," said Nick; "he had no trouble in doing as he pleased with us."

"But hogs go in droves, and you wouldn't be apt to find one of them by himself in the woods."

"There were others close by, for I am sure I heard them; but it is a little curious that they didn't attack us, for hogs don't know as much as dogs, and they had no reason to feel that one of their number was more than enough for us."

"I don't see the use in talking about it," remarked Herbert, who gently tipped his body to the other side, so as to rest differently on the ground; "I am sure I never was so upset in all my life."

"Nor were we," added Nick; "hogs are queer creatures; if a drove finds it is going to be attacked by an enemy, the boars will place themselves on the outside, with the sows and younger ones within, so as to offer the best resistance to the bear or whatever it is, and they will fight with great fury. In a wild state, they can run fast, and when the tusks of the boars get to be six or eight inches long, as they do in time, they are afraid of no animal in the woods."

"How is that?" asked Herbert, again shifting his position with great care, but feeling interested in what the lad was telling.

"I suppose because they haven't any reason to be afraid. With those frightful tusks curving upward from the lower jaw, and with a strength like Sampson in their necks, they can rip up a bear, a tiger, or any animal that dare attack them."

"I s'pose they're very strong, Nick?" continued Herbert.

"So strong, indeed, that one of the wild boars in Germany has run under the horse of a hunter, and, lifting both clear from the ground, trotted fifty yards with them, before the struggling animal could get himself loose."

Herbert looked fixedly at the narrator for a moment, then solemnly reached out his hand to Sam, for him to shake over the last astounding statement, which was altogether too much for him to credit.

Sam Harper grasped the hand and wabbled it once or twice, but said:

"It's as true as gospel, Herbert; I don't know anything about it myself, but when Nick Ribsam tells you anything for truth, you can make up your mind it is the truth and nothing else."

The friends lay for a long time by the camp fire, talking over the events of the day, while Nick Ribsam gave them many wonderful facts concerning the various wild animals found in different parts of the world. The lad read everything he could obtain relating to natural history, and his strong memory retained nearly all the facts.

But, as the night wore on, all three began to feel drowsy, and they made ready to sleep.

The arrangements for doing this were not so perfect as they could wish. Not one of them had anything like a blanket, and, though it was the time of the balmy Indian summer, the nights were quite cold.

There was an abundance of wood around them, and they gathered all they could possibly need. Then they heaped up a big lot of leaves and lay down as close to each other as possible.

This was the best that could be done; but it gave a great advantage to the one who lay in the middle, as the warmth of the others kept him comfortable, while they were forced to turn one side to the cold air.

By changing about, however, they got along quite well until past midnight, when the pile of leaves caught fire and caused them to leap to their feet with so much vigor that the outside ones got sufficiently warm to last till daylight.

The friends were glad enough when it began growing red in the east. They rose early, washed their hands and faces in the clear brook, which flowed near at hand, using their handkerchiefs for towels. Then a rabbit and couple of squirrels were shot, and, with the same wolf-like appetites, they made a nourishing and substantial meal.

The brook, from which they took a draught of clear, strengthening water, lay a short distance to the south of their camp, that is, between it and Shark Pond, which they passed the day before.

The three were standing by this stream, considering the best thing to be done to get on the track of the bear, when Sam Harper suddenly stopped talking and looked fixedly at a point a few yards away. Then he walked slowly to it, without removing his gaze, stooped down, and attentively scrutinized the ground.

Without speaking, he turned and beckoned to the others to approach.

CHAPTER XXVIII.

THE TRAIL OF THE BEAR.

The boys did as directed, and, also stooping down, saw in the soft earth near the water the prints of the feet of a large animal, such tracks indeed as could have been made only by the bear.

All agreed that it was that much desired and yet dreaded animal, and that it was more than likely he had moved to the southward, so that in point of fact the hunters and hunted had exchanged relative positions.

Sam sternly directed the attention of Bowser to the trail, and ordered him to "look into the matter."

The hound sniffed the ground, ran back and forth several times, and then gazed up at his master, as if awaiting further orders.

"I won't stand any such nonsense as that," said his impatient master, grasping him by the baggy skin at the back of the neck and giving him several sharp blows with a switch.

Bowser yelped and kicked lustily, and, when released, placed his nose to the ground, emitted several more cries, and then trotted off, taking a direction leading almost directly back over the path Herbert had followed the day before.

"He's on the trail *this* time," said Sam, with restored admiration for the hound, "and if he does well, I'll consider him a great deal better hunting dog than he has shown himself yet."

In fact, Bowser acted as if anxious to redeem his tainted reputation, and, trotting quite briskly, was soon out of sight among the trees, the lads hurrying after him.

A few minutes later, the yelping of the hound ceased, but the young hunters kept up their pursuit, the fresh trail made by the dog being easily followed, as he turned over and rumpled the abundant leaves on the ground, so that it was plainly discernible.

"I wonder why he has stopped barking," said Sam.

"I guess he has got tired," was the rather original reply of Herbert, who was ready to give information, whether reliable or not.

"Bowser seems to have a way of doing things which is different from other dogs—hallo! there he goes again."

The resounding cries of the hound echoed through the woods, seemingly at a distance of a half mile, and a little to the east of south.

"I guess he has treed him!" said Herbert, striking into a trot, the others doing the same, and very much doubting whether the odd dog had ever treed anything in his life.

A short run only was necessary, when, by stopping and listening, they learned that the hound was standing instead of running. If he had been a regular hunting dog, this fact would have proven that he had brought the game to bay.

As respecting Bowser, it was uncertain what it signified.

It did not take the lads long to hurry over the intervening space, when they came upon the hound, who was standing under a large red oak, looking up and barking with all the vigor he possessed.

"He has treed the bear, I do believe!" exclaimed Sam Harper, breaking ahead of the others in his excitement.

Nick Ribsam also thought the indications pointed that way.

CHAPTER XXIX.

"HELP! HELP!"

The belief that they were close upon the bear threw the boys into a flutter of excitement, and they walked slowly as they approached the tree, up which the hound was barking.

As has been stated, it was what was known as the red oak, very large, with branching limbs at no great distance from the ground.

"*I see him!—I see him!*" whispered Herbert, just as he caught his foot in a root and pitched forward.

"Where?"

Herbert picked up his hat, muttered something impatient, and then looked upward again, and found he was mistaken.

"I thought that big knot up there was the bear," replied the city youth, in meeker tones.

The boys slowly circled about the tree again and again, back and forth, scrutinizing trunk, limbs, and twigs so closely that a cat could not have concealed itself from view.

The result was disheartening: there was no bear in sight.

"May be the trunk is hollow," suggested Sam, "and he has gone into a hole."

They struck against the bark, but the sound showed that the wood beneath was solid. Besides, an examination of the bark itself failed to bring to view the scratching and abrasion that would have been made by a bear in going up, and especially in coming down, the trunk.

Bowser, beyond all question, had been "barking up the wrong tree."

"You're a pretty hunting dog, ain't you?" sneered Sam Harper, addressing the canine; "come here, that I may give you another switching."

But Bowser wheeled about, and, taking the trail again, trotted to the southward, his nose close to the ground, while he bayed at intervals of a few seconds.

"The bear ain't far off, you can make up your mind to that," said Herbert, still all excitement; "if we keep close to the dog, we'll run upon the other pretty soon."

In fact, the youthful Watrous showed such an interest in the sport that he forgot the danger which always accompanies it. Had he stopped a minute or so to reflect, he would have seen that now was the time for the three to stick together, for never was there likely to be an occasion which would demonstrate more certainly that in union there is strength.

Forgetful of this, Herbert sped forward so fast that in a brief while he vanished from view.

Nick shouted to him not to hasten so fast, but the young gentleman was not to be checked in that style, and he kept up his flight with undiminished speed.

"Let him go, then," said Nick, dropping down to a rapid walk, in which Sam joined him; "his legs are so long that he can outrun us both."

"Which is a good thing."

"Why so?"

"As soon as he catches sight of the bear, he will turn about and run with might and main."

"I'm not so sure of that," remarked Nick, who began to think there was more in Herbert than they had suspected.

"He is so anxious to get the animal that he doesn't know the risk he is running. The fight you had with the buck yesterday shows what a more harmless animal will do when he turns to fight the hunter."

"But Herbert will be likely to wait till we come up to him if he sees the bear."

"There's no telling what such a fellow will do when he loses his head; the only chance for him is that we may be so close that we can turn in and help him."

"Then we had better hurry."

Thereupon the two broke into a run again, which they kept up till pretty well tired out.

They could hear Bowser baying at no great distance, and, consequently, were sure that Herbert himself was not far off.

"If we three come upon him we ought to be able to kill him without much risk to ourselves—that is, if we use any sort of care in taking aim."

"We must try and do that—hark!"

At that instant they were startled by the sharp report of a rifle, the distance and direction leaving no doubt that it was fired by Herbert Watrous.

Sam and Nick fairly turned pale, and something like a feeling of envy came over them at the belief that Herbert, after all his boasting, had succeeded in bringing down the royal game without their help.

The shot was fired so close that, as they hastened forward again, they expected to come upon the hunter and his game every minute.

"Hallo! what does that mean?"

The question was caused by the sudden appearance of Bowser, who was limping toward them in a panic of terror. At every leap he uttered a yelp, which was of pain and fear.

The boys stopped, and the hound, running up, crouched down at their feet, whining and moaning.

"He is hurt!" said Sam, who noticed that he was bleeding from a wound in the shoulder, where the claws of some animal had struck him with great force.

"It was done by the bear," said Nick, "and he hit Bowser a hard blow; I shouldn't wonder if it kills him."

Sam stooped over the dog and tried to soothe him by patting and speaking kind words.

"He is badly hurt, but I hope he isn't going to die. Poor fellow! we have been unjust to him; he's a good deal braver dog than we gave him credit for."

They were still patting and soothing the wounded hound, when the report of Herbert's rifle was heard again. Sam and Nick started up and stared in the direction whence the sound came.

"He has got the bear—"

Just then the voice of Herbert was heard ringing through the forest arches:

"Quick! quick! help! help! the bear has got me! Hurry up, boys, or I'm a goner!"

The lads dashed forward, excited and fearful they would be too late.

The voice of the imperiled hunter rang out again.

"Quick! quick! the bear has got me sure! Hurry boys, hurry, for pity's sake!"

The next instant Sam and Nick came upon an extraordinary scene.

CHAPTER XXX.

A FRIEND IN NEED.

Herbert Watrous had been set upon by a huge bear, and, throwing aside his Creedmoor, had run with might and main for a large stump, behind which he took refuge. Had he climbed a sapling, he would have been safe, but he was too flustered to think of that.

Dodging behind this shelter he squatted down, hoping that his enemy did not notice where he had gone; but, when he heard the brute lumbering after him, he hastily shifted his quarters to the other side of the stump. While doing so, he emitted the ringing cries for help which brought his friends in such haste to his rescue.

The situation would have been laughable but for its element of peril. Darting to the side of the stump opposite to that of the bear, Herbert would drop his head, and then instantly pop up again, like a jack-in-the-box, to see what the brute was doing. The latter, it may be said, kept things moving.

When Herbert lowered his head and yelled, his voice had a muffled sound, as though it came from a distance, but when he shot up in sight, his cries were clear and distinct.

The beast, although heavy and awkward of movement, managed to move around the stump and to reverse his course with such facility that there can be little doubt that he would have caught the lad, had not his friends been so prompt to rush to his help.

Sam and Nick felt no disposition to laugh; indeed, they were so impressed by the danger that, without exercising the care they would have done any other time, and which they meant to show when talking of the matter a few minutes before, they raised their guns together and fired.

Although the aim was not as deliberate as it should have been, yet both bullets struck the bear, though neither inflicted a mortal wound.

The brute stopped short in his circular pursuit, looked confusedly about him for a second or two, and then made straight for the lads who had fired upon him, just as the buck did in the case of Nick Ribsam.

"Scatter and climb a tree!" called out Nick, who saw they had no chance to reload.

Now was the time for Herbert to recover, and reload his gun and to take another shot at the brute, so as to draw him off from his hot pursuit of the others; but the panic-stricken youth could not realize that the danger was removed, and that his terrible foe was bestowing his attention elsewhere. He continued calling for help in a louder voice than before, believing that every minute would be his last.

Sam Harper whirled about to make for a sapling, but caught his foot in an obstruction and fell violently to the ground. Nick was so alarmed that he stopped to help him up.

"I'm all right," said Sam, "look out for yourself!"

But Nick could not desert him, until assured he was not mangled by the fall, and by that time the bear was too close for them to escape by climbing a tree.

It looked as if it would go ill with one at least (for no gun in the party was loaded, and the brute was almost upon them), when most providentially, but unexpectedly, the report of another rifle broke upon their ear, and the bullet reached the heart of the monstrous beast, who reared himself on his haunches and used his paws as though trying to draw out the splinters which he imagined were thrust into his body.

Then he swerved to one side, sagged heavily to the ground, and then it was plain that all was over.

"Are any of you hurt?"

It was the voice of the plucky Mrs. Fowler, who hurried forward with anxious face, the smoking rifle in her hands.

Herbert was still peering from behind the stump and shouting himself hoarse, with no thought of what had taken place within the last few minutes. By and by, however, after he had been called to, he comprehended the facts and came forth, when a general explanation followed.

Although Herbert would not admit it, there was no doubt that of the two shots which he fired at the bear only one touched him, and that only to a sufficient extent to graze his body and to draw his attention to the young hunter.

Herbert then dropped his gun and made for the stump, which was not a secure refuge.

This took place so near the cabin-home of Mrs. Fowler that she heard the cries for help, and, taking down her rifle, hurried to the spot, arriving just in time to save the other lads from serious danger, if not from death.

The boys overwhelmed the brave woman with thanks, and though she modestly disclaimed her right to the bear—expressing her belief that the two shots they had fired were fatal—they would not listen to it, but they turned to, skinned the animal, and presented the hide to her, regretting that they had not several others, that her husband might collect twenty dollars apiece from Mr. Bailey, his employer.

"This isn't the only bear in the woods," said she, thanking them for their kindness; "and some of you will see another before long. But this will do for to-day."

They thought so, too; and, swinging their hats in the air, bade her good-by and started homeward.

Sam Harper proposed that they should go out of their path to examine the carcass of the deer, so as to learn whether the shot of Herbert took effect; but that young gentleman was frank enough to admit, after his experience, that it was impossible he had come anywhere near hitting the buck. Accordingly, they continued homeward, Herbert going back to the city a few days afterward to find out, if he could, why his gun so often failed to hit the object he aimed at.

CHAPTER XXXI.

THE "DARK DAY" OF SEPTEMBER, 1881.

The summer during which Nicholas Ribsam attained the age of twelve years was viewed with dismal forebodings by many people, for the reason that a celebrated weather prophet had foretold that it would be unusually rainy, cold, and wet.

As a consequence, it proved to be the driest known in years. Days, weeks, and even months passed without a drop of rain falling from the brassy sky, and the fine powdery dust permeated everywhere. The weather prophet lost caste, but he persisted in announcing rain, knowing that he had only to stick to it long enough to hit it in the course of time.

As the autumn approached and the drought continued over a vast extent of territory, the forest fires raged in different parts of the country. All day and night immense volumes of smoke and vapor hung over the land, and the appearance of the sun was so peculiar as to cause alarm on the part of those who were superstitious.

There came a "dark day," like that of the 19th of May, 1780, which overspread New England, and was most marked in Massachusetts. The Connecticut Legislature was in session, and the belief was so universal that the last awful day had come that the motion was made to adjourn. Then, as the graphic Quaker poet says:

All eyes were turned to Abraham Davenport.
He rose, slow cleaving with his steady voice
The intolerable hush. "This well may be
The Day of Judgment which the world awaits;
But be it so or not, I only know
My present duty, and my Lord's command
To occupy till He come. So at the post
Where He has set me in His providence,
I choose, for one, to meet Him face to face—
No faithless servant frightened from my task,
But ready when the Lord of the harvest calls;
And, therefore, with all reverence, I would say,
Let God do His work, we will see to ours.
Bring in the candles." And they brought them
in.

Tuesday, September 7, 1881, was a day very similar to the memorable one of a century ago. A strange, greenish-yellow pall overspread the heavens, and so darkened the light of the sun that lamps and gas were lighted, schools and factories closed, and multitudes of the ignorant and superstitious believed that the Day of Judgment had come.

Everything looked changed and unnatural. The faces of people on the streets were ghastly, the gas jets in the stores, instead of showing yellow, were as white and clear as the electric lights, and thousands of the sect known as Second Adventists gathered in their places of worship and confidently awaited the appearing of the Lord.

The "dark day" was more wonderful in the country. The leaves and withering foliage assumed a most singular tint of green, changing, like that of the grass, to a brownish hue; fowls went to roost, and the animal creation must have been greatly mystified by a phenomenon such as they had never witnessed before.

A curious feature of this luminous haze was that it cast no shadow. It was as light under the trees as away from them, the whole unnatural appearance of things most likely being due to the immense forest fires which were raging in many parts of the country.

It was during the summer, I repeat, in which Nick Ribsam reached the age of twelve years, that so many forest fires raged, and it was in the autumn of the same year that he saw the famous dark day, so similar to that of September, 1881; in fact, it could not have resembled it more closely, for I may as well state it was that very day to which I refer.

"Nick," said his father, on that September morning, addressing his boy in Dutch, "I promised to pay James Bradley one hundred dollars to-day before three o'clock."

"Yes, sir," responded the boy, who knew that the debt would be paid on time.

"He was to come here to our house to get it, but he sent me word last night that he would be much obliged if I would send it to him at Martin's store in Dunbarton, as he is obliged to be there all day. I like to accommodate any one, and I will therefore send you to take it to him."

"Yes, sir; I am ready to go whenever you want me to do so."

Dunbarton, as has been stated, was a village nine miles away, and the principal grocery store in the place was kept by Jacob Martin. It was there that Nick was to take the one hundred dollars which was to be handed to James Bradley, to whom his father owed it.

It was like a holiday for Nick to take such a drive, and he was glad when his father made known his wishes.

"Harness up the mare to the fall-top and drive over; you ought to be back early in the afternoon."

"I will, if nothing happens to prevent."

Just then rosy-faced Nellie came out to feed the chickens. As the fowls flocked toward her, some perching on her shoulders, head, and wherever they could find a resting-place, she scattered the golden grains of corn with a deft and lavish hand.

Her father looked at the cheeks as red as apples and the eyes glowing with health, and, dropping into English, said with a sigh and shake of the head:

"I dinks dot Nellie looks some bale."

He meant to say pale, and Nick laughed.

"I don't think she is very sick; she ate more breakfast than I did this morning."

"Dot ish so, but I dinks dot I leafes her go mit you to Dunbarton, if she can shpare her moder."

Mr. Ribsam meant all right, and when his wishes were made known to Nellie she was delighted; her mother was glad to give her the privilege of an excursion, for she was an industrious little girl, and, furthermore, there were some purchases to be made both for the mother and daughter, which Nellie could attend to better than could any boy, no matter how intelligent.

The famous "dark day" of 1881 prevailed principally in New England and the State of New York; but it was noticed further south, especially in some of the wooded portions of Pennsylvania, though in the larger part of the commonwealth it attracted no great attention.

It was between seven and eight o'clock when the four-wheeled carriage with the single seat, and which vehicle is known as a "fall top" in some sections of the country, was driven from the humble home of the Ribsams, with the brother and sister seated in it.

As they approached the scene of Nellie's adventure with the bear, they naturally talked about it, while Nick again related his own thrilling experience, when the animal was shot by Mrs. Fowler, just in the nick of time.

Shark Creek had suffered so much from the long continued drought that it was no more than one fourth its usual volume; but the pond below was not much diminished in size, as it did not flow off except when at a certain height.

The brother and sister did not speak of the peculiar appearance of the atmosphere until nearly to the bridge. There had been a great deal of smoke floating over the country for several days, but there was nothing to cause any fear on the part of those who lived near the large stretches of timber.

As the darkness increased, however, Nick said:

"It must be caused by the thick smoke; but I don't think it will last, and when we reach Dunbarton that will be the end of it."

"It won't make any difference," said Nellie, "unless it gets so dark we can't see the way."

"No fear of that."

But when at last they emerged from the woods, and shortly after entered the village, the impressive gloom was deeper than ever. The villagers were awed by the unnatural appearance of nature, and were standing in groups looking at the sky and talking in undertones.

Many were frightened, and not a few hurried to their homes, terrified with the belief that the last awful day, when the heavens shall be burned up as a scroll and the elements shall melt with fervent heat, was at hand.

Ah, had it been the final Judgment Day, how many of us would have had our houses in order for the coming of the angel of the Lord?

Nick Ribsam sprang out of the carriage, helped Nellie to alight, and went into the store of Mr. Martin, where James Bradley was found awaiting him. The money was handed over, a receipt taken, the horse fed, during which Nellie attended to the errand on which she was sent, and, an hour later, the mare was given water, and brother and sister started homeward, little dreaming of what awaited them.

CHAPTER XXXII.

THE BURNING FOREST.

"It is growing darker all the time."

"So it seems; I never saw anything like it."

"Maybe it is really night, Nick, and we have lost our reckoning. Isn't there any way by which the world might swing out of its—what do you call it?"

"Orbit, I suppose, you mean; there may be such a way, but from what I have studied, when it does do that there will be more of a disturbance than simple darkness like this."

These words were exchanged between brother and sister after they had penetrated the woods a considerable distance on their return home. It had become like night around them, except that, as has been shown, the gloom was of that peculiar lurid nature which can hardly be described, and can never be forgotten by those who saw it.

Even Nick Ribsam was impressed. It could not have been otherwise, for any one would have been lacking in natural sensibility had he failed to be awed by the singular sight. It can scarcely be said that the lad was frightened, although there came over him a yearning feeling that he might hurry home so the family could all be together, if the awful calamity—whatever it might be—should descend.

It was different with the sister Nellie; her nature was more impressible, and it was only by a strong effort that she kept her self-control so long. As she peeped furtively out from the carriage, she looked at the woods, penetrated by the strange haze, which perhaps took on a more striking appearance in an autumnal forest like that, than anywhere else.

"Nick, I believe it's the Last Day that has come."

The lad turned toward his sister, who was sitting far back in her seat, as though trying to shut out the scene which had such a fascination for her.

The face of the girl wore such a ghastly color, that Nick could not wonder at her fright, but he shook his head. He felt he was the man now, and it would not do for him to show any weakness.

"It isn't the Judgment Day, Nellie; for, according to the Bible, it will come in a different way than this. There are a good many things which are not understood by folks, and I suppose this must be one of them."

"I can smell burning wood," broke in the sister, leaning forward and snuffing the smoky air.

"I am sure I do, and that's what is making all this trouble."

"But suppose, Nick, these woods are on fire? How far is it back to where we entered them?"

"About three miles, and it is five to the open country ahead, where we leave them; but there is the creek, less than a mile ahead, so if we should find the woods burning, we can stop there till it is over."

The sister, however, had suggested a danger to the brother which alarmed him. The mare had been walking slowly, for it seemed more in harmony with the scene that she should do so. The driver now jerked the lines so sharply that she pricked up her ears and started off at a rapid gait, that is as the mare herself doubtless looked upon traveling.

The first real thrill of alarm came to the lad, when he recalled that if a fire should appear, he and his sister were in the worst possible position: there were three miles of forest behind and five in front.

The mare seemed to awaken to a sense of danger, for she threw up her head with unusual sprightliness, struck into a trot so rapid that Nick was a little frightened, lest in the gloom the carriage should come in contact with some obstruction which he could not detect in time.

"See there!"

As Nellie uttered the exclamation, she caught the arm of her brother and pointed ahead, but there was no need of her doing so, for he had seen the peril. The road immediately in front was filled with heavy smoke, which, as it rolled forward, caused them to cough almost to the strangulation point. At the same time, a crimson streak of flame shot in and out of the murky vapor, like the flashing of lightning: the fire was burning immediately in front and it would not do to go further.

Nick stopped the horse, and, half rising and bending forward, peered into the suffocating vapor. Then he turned and looked behind him, in which direction Nellie was also gazing.

"How is it there?" he asked.

"There is plenty of smoke, but I see no fire."

"Then we must go back."

The road was quite narrow, though there was room for two teams to pass each other, and Nick turned the frightened mare as quickly as he could; she was so nervous and fidgety that it was hard work to control her, but she was headed toward Dunbarton, after some difficulty, and as soon as the rein was given her, away she went at a spanking trot.

But neither the brother nor sister was relieved of fear, for the smoke grew denser every minute, and Nick might well ask himself whether he would be able to pass the three miles before he could reach the safety of the open country.

The question was answered much sooner than he anticipated. The sharp crackling was heard, and they caught glimpses of the fiery tongues leaping in and out among the dried leaves and vegetation on either hand. Suddenly the flames seemed to meet in front in such a rushing, roaring volume that it was vain to think of pushing any further in the face of it.

"Oh, Nick," moaned Nellie, shrinking close to him, "we are going to be burned alive!"

"It does look bad, Nellie, but we mustn't give up yet; one thing is certain, it won't do to try to reach Dunbarton to-day."

"But we can't go homeward."

"It doesn't look so bad that way as it does toward Dunbarton: we must try one of the roads, and I would rather work toward home than away from it."

Nick was busy while talking; he saw that the mare was becoming panic-stricken, and it required all his strength and firmness to keep her from breaking away from him.

"O Nick," moaned Nellie, "we are going to be burned alive."

By using the whip, he managed to turn her again in the road, and then he struck her sharply with the lash.

"Nellie, catch hold of my arm," he said to her, feeling that even if everything came out in the best form, a severe struggle was before them.

The mare sniffed, and, glancing to her right and left, gave a whinny of terror as she dropped into her swiftest trot, which, a minute after, she changed to a gallop; but Nick brought her down instantly to her more natural gait.

Nellie slipped her arm under the elbow of her brother, and then clasped her two hands, so as to hold fast for the shock which she believed would soon come.

A large branch had fallen across the road, and Nick did not catch sight of it until too late to check the flying mare. The carriage seemed to bound fully a foot into the air, and an ominous wrench told the driver that it had suffered material damage.

But there was no time to stop and examine; the terrified horse sprang into a gallop again, and this time Nick did not restrain her.

There was smoke all around them; the air was hot and suffocating; they could hear the crackling of flames, and now and then the crimson flash through the murky vapor showed that a frightful forest fire was raging on every hand.

Still the mare kept forward at the same swift gallop, and Nick knew that more than once she felt the blistering heat on her haunches. It is a strange peculiarity of the horse, which often shows a wonderful degree of intelligence, that he generally loses his wits when caught in a conflagration. Instead of running away from the flames he often charges among them, and there remains, fighting those who are trying to save him.

Very probably the mare would have acted similarly in the instance of which I am speaking had the circumstances permitted it; but there was fire all about her, and the temptation was as strong, therefore, in one direction as another.

Nick kept his self-possession. He knew by the desperate energy with which Nellie clung to his arm that she was helpless, and that every minute they were likely to plunge headlong into and among the roaring flames.

He could not guide the mare, which was now controlled by her own instinctive desire to escape a danger which was on every hand. He merely sought to direct her, so far as possible, in the hope that he might save the carriage from being dashed to pieces.

When he saw the flames meeting across the road he shouted to Nellie to hold her breath, and he did the same, until they had swept through the fiery, strangling ring, and were able to catch a mouthful of the smoky and scorching atmosphere beyond.

CHAPTER XXXIII.

THROUGH THE FIRE.

It was hard to remain cool when surrounded by such peril as were Nick and Nellie Ribsam but the sturdy lad acquitted himself like a hero.

His belief was that all the woods were not on fire—that is, the entire tract was not burning at once, and that, as a consequence, if he could break through the flaming circle in which he was caught, he could place himself and sister in front of the danger, so to speak, and then they would be able to run away from it altogether.

If such were the case, it followed that just then speed was the most important of all things, and for that reason he kept the mare on her sweeping gallop, at the imminent risk of dashing the carriage to pieces every minute.

He was glad that he did not meet any vehicles, for it not only showed that no one else in the neighborhood was placed in the same extremity as were he and his sister, but it lessened the danger of collision.

Nick thought it was all over with them, when a fiery serpent, as it seemed, darted across from one side of the road to the other, directly in front. It was at the height of five or six feet, and coiling itself about a dry pine it shot horizontally toward another pine, wrapped with a flaming girdle, which sent out a line of fire to meet it, like the intense blaze seen when a blow-pipe is used.

It was a curious manifestation, and it would be hard to explain it, for, though a strong wind was blowing, that would not account for the fact that the two tongues of fire, as they really were, met each other in this fashion across the road, for of a necessity they extended themselves in opposite directions.

They did not burn steadily, but whisked back and forth, just as it may be imagined two serpents would have done who saw the fugitives coming, and, making ready, said by their actions, "Thus far, but no farther."

To Nick Ribsam it looked like the flaming sword of Hazael, sweeping across the highway; but it would never do to hesitate, and the mare galloped straight on. The fiery serpents darted angrily at each other, but the head of the horse glided beneath and the boy caught a hot blast as he shot by.

"Where is the bridge?" shouted Nellie, who could see nothing, and who clung more desperately than ever to the supporting arm of her brother.

"It must be close at hand—there it is!"

So it was, indeed, but the fire was ahead of them; the whole structure was one mass of flames, roaring and crackling with fury.

The scene that followed was a dreadful one: the sight of the furnace-like structure set the mare wild, and she broke into a dead run toward the blazing mass of kindling wood, determined to plunge headlong into it.

Nick Ribsam rose to his feet, and bent back with might and main, but he might as well have tried to check a runaway locomotive: the mare took the bit in her teeth and was beyond control.

With a presence of mind which did him credit, Nick wrenched her to one side, while she was at the height of this mad flight, so that the hub of the fore wheel struck a tree at the side of the road, checking the vehicle so abruptly that both traces snapped as if they were ribbons, and the mare continued her gallop in the direction of the bridge.

The momentum of Nellie threw her violently against the dashboard, while Nick, before he could let go the reins, was jerked out the carriage, and, lighting on his feet, ran a dozen steps ere he could check himself and free his hands from the reins.

He stopped almost on the edge of the creek, and caught one glimpse of the mare as she bounded out of sight into the smoke and flames, and was gone forever.

The lad felt a pang of sorrow for the foolish beast, who stood as good a chance of saving herself as he, had she but used a tithe of common sense; but there was no time for mourning, and he ran back to the vehicle, where Nellie was crouching, and crying violently.

"Why, Nellie, I am ashamed of you!" said her brother, reprovingly. "Is it going to mend matters to sit down and cry?"

"But how can I help it, Nick?" she asked, rubbing her red eyes with her apron and trying to check herself; "I don't see how you can keep from crying yourself!"

"I'm glad I ain't such a ninny as you, and when I get home I am going to tell father and mother."

"You needn't be so smart," said Nellie, beginning to fire up under the reproof of her brother; "you haven't got home yet."

"And mighty little chance I would stand of ever getting there if I should sit down like you and begin to blubber. Come out of the carriage and go with me."

Nellie's face was very red and there were tears on her cheeks, her countenance wearing a strange appearance in the lurid haze around them.

The girl did not make any objection, for she could not do otherwise than lean on the strong arm of her brother, who never seemed to lose his head over anything. Every minute or so a distressing feeling came over them—such a feeling as we can imagine would be ours were we suddenly to find ourselves shut in a room where the air was so impure we could not breathe it.

There was a gasping, hurried inhalation of the strangling hot smoke—a coughing and filling of the eyes with tears, and then a frantic rush of several steps, during which the breath was held until a chance to get a mouthful of fresh air was gained.

It was useless to turn back. The children were in the very heart of the wood, and the conflagration was raging so furiously on both sides, and in front and rear, that it was impossible to escape in either direction.

But for the timely arrival at the edge of the creek they must have perished a few minutes later, and they could not feel certain as yet that even water would save them.

The creek was so low, that when they hurriedly picked their way down the bank to it, Nick could have taken Nellie on his back and carried her across without wetting her feet; but there was nothing to be gained by doing so, as the fire was burning as fiercely on one side as on the other.

The conflagration must stop when it should reach the margin of the stream, and Nick drew a sigh of relief, feeling that they were safe.

"We will wait here till the fire is done burning," said he, standing with the hand of his sister in his own, while he gazed about him on the extraordinary scene.

The day had been quite warm, and Nick and Nellie, pausing on the bank of the shrunken creek, began to find themselves exceedingly uncomfortable; for not only was there a great increase of heat, but the smoke was too heavy to be breathed without great pain and irritation to the lungs.

"It looks as if we are to be strangled to death, after all," Nick said, "for it is hard to breathe now, and it is growing worse every minute."

"Let's go up by the pond: it isn't far away."

"It must be as bad there as anywhere else, but we shall die if we stay here."

There seemed little choice in the matter, but one of the impossibilities is for a boy or girl to stand still when suffering, and the suggestion of Nellie was acted upon at once.

She had released the arm of Nick, who started up the right bank, she following close behind him. The walking was easy, for the creek had receded from the greater portion of the bed it usually occupied, and that had become hardened by long exposure to the heat of the sun.

It was not far to the pond of which I have spoken, and which occupied an extent of an acre, or perhaps more. The place was a favorite with the boys of the neighborhood, and some of the most delightful swims Nick Ribsam had ever enjoyed were in that sheet of water.

The water was cold, clear, and deep in many places. What more tempting resort for a tired, thirsty and overheated lad can be imagined especially when he knows that it will be a piece of disobedience for him to go there?

"That's the place," he exclaimed, hastening his footsteps; "when we get there, we'll have a chance to breathe."

"Hurry up, then, Nick, for I can't stand this much longer."

CHAPTER XXXIV.

CALLING IN VAIN.

The distress of the brother and sister became greater every minute. They walked hurriedly along the bank of the creek, their path through the gloom illuminated now and then by the flashes of fire which shot through the strangling volumes of vapor. Nick, more than likely, would have gone astray but for his familiarity with the neighborhood.

It seemed to him as if the smoke, heavy, dense, sulphurous and suffocating, caused by the burning forest, was driven toward the bed of the stream, where it was pressed down by the weight from above, until it was the utmost he and Nellie could do to inhale enough of the contaminated air to sustain life.

They hurried and struggled forward as best they could, and at last caught the glimmer of the broad expanse of water, which presented itself in the light of a haven of refuge to them.

It was a most welcome relief indeed, for they were now assured of one thing —they could not die the frightful death that overtook the poor mare. This broad expanse of cool, refreshing water could not burn up, no matter how fervent the heat that might envelop its shores. Its cool depths offered a refreshing refuge, such as can hardly be understood by one who is not suffering similarly.

But it was rather curious that the boy and girl had endured more from the suffocating vapor than from the fire itself. Looking down at their garments, they were surprised to find them scorched in several places, and Nellie gave just the faintest scream when a pungent odor directed her gaze to a large hole burning in her dress.

Nick glanced around, and, understanding what the matter was, called rather sharply:

"Pinch it out!"

She was already doing so, and she asked:

"Why don't you pinch out that fire on your coat?"

Just then her brother jumped into the air and shouted, "Oh—ouch!" for the burning sleeve had gone through the shirt and reached the bare skin. He whipped off his coat in a twinkling, dipped it hastily into the water, doing the same with his right elbow, the element which extinguished the smoking garment being very grateful to the scorched limb.

"Nellie," said he, "just cast your eye over me, and let me know whether there are any more fires going."

He made up his mind that if she reported other conflagrations breaking out, he would subdue them in a lump by taking a header in the pond, whose shore they reached at that moment. But Nellie said he was in no danger so far as she could see, of immediate combustion and when she came to examine her own garments they were also free from the same peril.

"Now, what shall we do that we have got here?" she asked, as, after walking a few steps, he came to a stop.

"Wait, and see how things are coming out," he answered. "I begin to feel tired, so suppose we sit down and rest ourselves."

The moment this was done, both uttered an exclamation of pleasure; for the relief from the distressing smoke was so great that it was as if they had emerged into the open country, where there was none of it at all.

"Why did we not think of this before?" said Nick; "we ought to have known that smoke doesn't keep close to the ground."

The atmosphere was not clear by any means, but the change was so marked that it appeared more than pure, and they sat several minutes gratefully inhaling that from which it seemed they had been shut off for many hours.

But their rejoicing was too soon; for, though it may be true that in a burning building the surest place in which to gain enough air to support life is close to the floor, yet there can be so much of the strangling vapor that it will penetrate everywhere.

Less than five minutes had passed, when a volume of smoke swept over and enveloped them, so dense that it was like the darkness of Egypt, that could be felt, and the suffering of the brother and sister was pitiful.

"Put your face close to the water," called out Nick, as well as he could do from coughing and strangling.

At the same moment, their fevered cheeks touched the cold, refreshing surface, and something of relief was experienced.

"It won't do to stay here," said Nick, a moment later.

"But where can we go?"

"Out in the pond; there's a better chance to breathe there than along shore."

"But I can't swim, Nick."

"What of that? I can, and I'll take care of you; but there is plenty of wood and we can make a raft. That reminds me that there *was* a raft here last week, when Sam Harper and I had a swim: I wonder where it can be. Help me to look for it."

They moved slowly along the margin of the pond, peering through the gloom as best they could, but seeing nothing of the support on which they now placed so much hope.

Nick Ribsam, however, did not fail to notice one thing—it was becoming hotter every minute and they could not wait much longer before entering the water in very self-defense.

They pushed bravely on, and when the circuit of Shark Pond was half completed, reached a point where the thick vapor lifted, or, more properly, it had not yet descended, and they stopped to rest themselves again.

"Well," exclaimed Nick, with a sigh, "some folks would call this fun, but I don't see where it comes in."

"I don't see how any one could find fun in such suffering; but, Nick, you will have to make a raft."

"I believe you are right; there isn't much chance to fasten these dry logs together, and I haven't time to build one that will hold us both."

"What will you do?"

"I will place you on it, and I'll swim along-side——"

"There's the raft! I see it! I see it!"

Nellie sprang to her feet and pointed out on the pond where, through the smoky gloom, the outlines of the half dozen logs, which Nick and several of his playmates had bound together with withes, when frolicking in the water, were seen.

The lad threw off his hat, vest, shoes, and stockings, so that only his shirt and trousers remained, and then took a header, his whole being thrilling with pleasure as the cold water closed around him.

"Take care of my clothes!" he called to Nellie, "and I'll bring the raft over to you."

As there was no immediate hurry, the situation of his sister being quite comfortable, the lad could not resist the temptation to disport himself awhile in the cool, refreshing element. He sank until his bare feet touched the pebbly bottom, and then shot upward with a bound; then he went over backward, floundered, and tumbled about like a porpoise.

"Nick," called his sister, "you had better hurry and get that raft, for I cannot see it now."

This startled the lad, but when he found he could not see Nellie either, he understood that it was on account of the overshadowing gloom that had fallen still lower; at the same time the disturbance of the atmosphere had caused a strong wind to blow across the pond, and it was doubtless this which had started the mass of pine logs from the land, and was now bearing it away from where it lay when discovered by the girl.

"Are you comfortable there?" called out Nick to his sister.

"Yes, but don't wait too long, for it is growing warm, and I think the fire is close to me."

The lad felt he had done wrong in idling his time, and he bent all his energies toward swimming to the raft, which, under any circumstances could not be far off.

As it was, Nick was amazed to find it necessary to go a considerable ways before he caught sight of the familiar pile of logs floating buoyantly on the water, but he speedily reached them, and, drawing himself on top, hunted for the long pole that he had used so many times in navigating the pond.

But it was not there, and he sank back into the water, and, holding on with his hands, used his feet vigorously to propel the raft toward the bank, where he had left his loved sister but a short time before.

"I'll soon be there, Nellie," he called; "are you all right?"

This was a curious question to ask, though it was natural, perhaps, for any boy, under similar circumstances, but Nick felt a pang of fear when he repeated the call and did not receive any answer.

He put forth all the energy at his command, and steadily pushed the float toward land. Now and then, while doing so, he shouted to his sister, without hearing any reply.

"Can it be anything has happened to her?" he asked himself several times as he peered through the gloom, unable to catch the outlines of brave little Nellie.

CHAPTER XXXV.

WHAT FRIGHTENED NELLIE.

Nick Ribsam thought not of himself, in his anxiety for his sister. He had left her but a few brief minutes before, sitting on the shore of the lake, and now when he returned she was missing.

He had called to her repeatedly without receiving any answer, and when he looked about him in the smoke and gloom, he could see nothing of her loved figure.

He noticed that it was very hot where he stood, and there could be no doubt that the flames were advancing in that direction. His dread was that Nellie had lost her wits in the presence of the new danger, and had run blindly into the burning woods where there could be no escape for her.

"Nellie! Nellie!" he shouted in agonized tones; "Where are you? Why don't you answer me?"

He thought he heard something like a faint response, but it was not repeated, and poor Nick was half distracted. For the first time since entering the burning forest he lost his self-control, and not doubting that his sister was somewhere close at hand, he dashed among the trees, still calling to her at the height of his voice.

He had gone but a short distance when he was brought face to face with such a fierce blast of flame that he was forced to turn and run back to the water's edge, where he stopped for a minute or two gasping for breath.

This repulse served to give him time to collect his wits, and he tried hard to decide what was best to do, for he was resolved never to leave that place until he learned the fate of Nellie.

"She had good sense," he added to himself, "and she would not have done such a foolish thing. She has gone to some other spot along the shore and is waiting for me."

Possibly this was so, but it did not explain the curious fact that all the calls of Nick remained unanswered. The space inclosing the pond was so slight that his voice must have penetrated every portion of it, and it did seem that if she were in any place safe for her to be, she could not fail to hear him.

Nick found a long branch, which answered for a pole with which to guide the raft, and stepping on it he began pushing it along shore as rapidly as he could, looking into the gloom about him and often pronouncing the name of his sister. His heart sank within him when this continued several minutes, and half the circuit of the pond was completed without bringing him the first evidence of the whereabouts of Nellie.

Finally he paused, wearied and distressed beyond description.

The darkness of night rested on Shark Pond and the surrounding woods. The murky volumes of smoke seemed to shut out all light, excepting when the tongues of fire shot through them. The wind blew a gale, stirring the water into tiny waves, and the roaring of the fire through the woods, the sound of trees crashing to the earth, and the millions of sparks, with blazing bits of wood, were carried a great distance through the air. Some of these flaming brands fell on the raft on which Nick Ribsam stood, and they continually dropped hissing into the water around him.

The problem was, how the children had escaped thus far; and as the sturdy lad stood out on the pond with the long limb grasped in his hand, staring around him, he could not but wonder how it was he had been preserved after driving directly into the forest when it was literally aflame from one end to the other.

But these thoughts were only for the moment; he had left Nellie, not expecting to be out of her sight, much less beyond her hearing, and she had vanished as mysteriously as if the earth had opened and swallowed her up.

And yet he could not believe she was lost. She had proven that she was not the weak girl to do anything rashly, or to sit down and fold her hands and make no attempt to save herself. Something more than the general danger which impended over both must have arisen, during that brief period, to drive her from her post.

"Nellie! Nellie!" he called again, shoving the pole vigorously against the bottom of the pond.

He was sure he heard the faint response this time, and so distinctly that he caught the direction; it was from a point on the shore very nearly opposite where he had left her.

"I hear you," he called back, working the unwieldy float toward the spot; "I'll soon be there."

The distance was not great and it took but a few minutes to approach quite close to the land, where, with a delight which can scarcely be imagined, he saw Nellie standing close to the water's edge, beckoning him to make all haste.

"Are you hurt?" he asked, as he forced the craft close to her.

"No," she answered, with a strange laugh, "but I thought my last moment had come."

"Didn't you hear me call you?"

"Of course I did; any one within a mile could hear you."

"Why then didn't you answer me?"

"I was afraid to."

"Afraid of what?"

"Didn't you see him?" was the puzzling question of Nellie in return, as she stepped carefully upon the raft, helped by the extended hand of her brother.

"Nellie, stop talking in puzzles," said Nick; "I was so scared about you that I won't get over it for a week; I called to, and hunted for you, and you say you heard me; you must have known how frightened I was, and yet you stood still and never made any answer, except a minute ago, when I just managed to hear you. If you think it is right, I don't—that's all."

He turned away offended, when she said:

"Forgive me, Nick; but I was afraid to answer you."

"Afraid of *what*?"

"Of that *bear*—you must have seen him," was the astonishing answer of the girl.

Nellie then told her story: she was standing on the shore awaiting the return of her brother, when she was terrified almost out of senses by the appearance of a large black bear, which was evidently driven out of the burning forest by the flames.

He did not seem to notice the girl, but when he began lumbering toward her, as if seeking a good spot where he might enter the pond, Nellie did not stay on the order of her going, but fled from the new peril, hardly conscious of what direction she took. She knew better than to venture among the blazing trees from which she and her brother had had such a narrow escape, and she sped forward around the lake until she reached a point nearly opposite. On the way she never looked behind her once, certain as she was that the creature was ready to seize and devour her.

She was sure she heard him crashing almost upon her heels; but when she paused, and finally turned her frightened looks backward, nothing of the brute was to be seen, and she did not know what had become of him.

"That's the other bear which Mrs. Fowler saw, and which she told Sam Harper, Herbert Watrous, and me, we would see some time or other."

"But that was almost two years ago."

"I know that; don't you suppose a bear will keep that long? This one has known enough to stay out of sight until the fire has forced him from his hiding-place."

After Nellie had heard her brother call to her, she was fearful that if she answered she would betray herself to the brute, who would instantly make for her; so she held her peace, even though she saw nothing of the bear, and venturing on a rather feeble answer when the tones of Nick told how much apprehension he was suffering over his failure to find her.

Now that the two were on the raft, which was shoved out in the deep water, something like confidence came back to her, and she was willing to talk about the beast.

"I can't imagine what has become of him," said the brother, after her story was told; "from what I have heard and read, the bear is not afraid of water, and they often go in to bathe, just like us boys, for the fun of the thing. I don't see why he should have waited when he had the fire to urge him on."

"Maybe he is swimming around the lake now," whispered Nellie, looking over as much of the surface as was visible through the hot smoke.

"I shouldn't be surprised, though it is odd that I did not see him," said Nick, pressing his pole against the bottom; "he is not far off, you may depend."

"There! didn't you hear him?" asked Nellie, a moment later, as something like the grunt of a huge hog alarmed both brother and sister.

CHAPTER XXXVI.

AN UNWELCOME PASSENGER.

A second time a loud snort was heard, as though some large animal were blowing the water from his nostrils, and at the same instant Nick and Nellie caught sight of the huge snout of the bear coming through the water toward them.

He was making directly for the raft beyond all question.

"By jingo, this raft wasn't built to carry bears!" exclaimed the startled lad, who used the pole with all the strength of which he was master; but, unfortunately, the bottom of the pond was composed of slippery rocks in many places, and the blunt end of the crooked limb slid along the upper surface of one of these so quickly that Nick dropped on his side and came within a hair's breadth of rolling overboard.

But he was up again like a flash, and toiling with might and main.

Rafts as generally constructed, are not capable of much speed, and though Nick Ribsam got out all there was in the one which he had managed, it was not to be expected that he could compare with the velocity of a strong, healthy bear.

"He's coming, Nick! Oh, he will catch us sure!" exclaimed the sorely frightened Nellie, edging so far away that she, too, was in danger of going over.

"I know he is," replied the sturdy lad, working hard with the guiding pole, "and I think he can beat us. Do you stay where you are, and don't try to get any further off or you will be drowned. I'll bang him over the head if he tries to climb on here and ride with us."

Such was the purpose of the beast, beyond question; and, approaching fast, only a brief time elapsed ere his huge snout was shoved against the logs, his big paws, dripping with wet, flapped out from below the surface and both rested on the raft, which sank so low that Nellie screamed and Nick turned pale.

Determined to keep off such an undesirable passenger, the lad raised the stick in his hand and brought it down with all his strength on the head of the bear, which acted as though unaware that he was struck.

Nick repeated the blows, that would have settled the business for a less formidable animal but it was plain that brain did not consider the matter a serious one. Having secured a rest for his paws, his whole body was supported in the water, and the beast, which was no doubt very tired, simply ceased all effort, and floated with the wind.

"Why don't you knock him off?" asked Nellie, impatiently.

"Because I ain't strong enough, I suppose; he's the toughest customer I ever got hold of, or seemed to have a good chance to get hold of me."

"I've a great notion to dig out his eyes myself."

"If you try it, it will be the last bear you ever scratch; look at those paws! did you ever see such nails? didn't you hear them rattle against the logs when he struck them?"

"Suppose he tries to climb upon the raft," ventured Nellie, trying to edge still further away, "what will become of us?"

"The raft won't hold him; he'll sink it, and we'll have to get along as best we can; but, Nellie, he acts to me as though he is satisfied with being where he is, and he won't disturb us so long as we let him alone."

"But you struck him several hard blows."

"He's forgotten all about it, if he ever knew it. I guess he has had a pretty lively run to reach the pond in time to save his hide, and now that he is in the water, he will stay there a good while."

120

There was a likelihood that Nick was right, and that the bear wanted nothing more than a rest; and yet the possibility that he would soon try to draw his entire body upon the raft prevented the brother and sister from having any peace of mind.

When this singular tableau had lasted several minutes, it was discovered that the wind was carrying the raft, with its incubus, toward the western shore again, and Nick, afraid that if they all landed together, the bear might seize the occasion to make a supper off of them, reached the pole over the side, and began working the logs to the middle of the pond.

During this performance the brute never stirred. His head, shoulders and paws were out of the water, the principal bulk of his body being beneath, and he seemed contented to be navigated about the small lake in any fashion the proprietor of the raft deemed best.

When considerable time had passed without his offering to destroy them, the boy and girl were able to view the beast with feelings of less alarm. They looked at the large head, pig-like snout, round, dark eyes, and could well understand the terror which an unarmed person feels on meeting one of them in the woods.

But so long as bruin remained there, so long was he a threat; and Nick was trying hard to think of some plan by which to get rid of him.

He had tested beating him, but with no success, while he ran the risk of exciting him to a dangerous degree of savagery if he should persist in it. The boy had no weapon about him, unless his jack-knife should be counted as such, and nothing could be accomplished with that. He asked himself whether it were possible to dive under the raft and give him two or three vigorous thrusts with the implement; but, fortunately, the lad had too much sense to undertake anything of that sort, which, more than likely, would have resulted in the destruction of himself and sister.

There really seemed no way open for the young hero to do anything at all, except to follow the advice of his father: "Do all you can for yourself and then leave the rest to Providence."

"If I could think of anything," said he to Nellie, "I would do it, but we shall have to wait."

"Maybe when he is rested he will swim off and go ashore."

"I wish he would; but it seems to me that he has got a look in his eye, which says that pretty soon he will try to enjoy a little more of the raft than he now does: and when he undertakes it, you can make up your mind, Nellie, that there will be a row."

"Why not let the raft drift close to land, so as to give him a chance to get off?" she asked.

"Suppose he doesn't take the chance, which he has now; no, we'll wait awhile and see what he thinks about it."

So soon as they could feel anything like relief from watching the passenger, the brother and sister looked at the scene around them, which was enough to strike any one with awe.

The murky vapor was pouring across the water; burning leaves, sticks, and large branches of wood seemed to be carried almost horizontally on the wind, while the blazing forest roared like the ocean when swept by the monsoon.

Whether the memorable dark day of 1881 still overspread the earth beyond, the two had no means of knowing; but they did know and feel that they were enveloped in an awful night, illumined only by the burning forests about them.

Should the bear fail to harm them, they might well ask themselves the question, when would they be able to leave the water, in which they had taken refuge. It was not likely they would be forced to keep to the raft itself very long, but, after stepping foot on shore, they would be surrounded, if not by the burning forest itself, by its embers, which would render traveling perilous for days to come.

Altogether, it will be seen that the situation of the two was as unpleasant—if, not absolutely dangerous—as it could well be.

Nick was on the point, more than once, of following the advice of his sister,— to allow the raft to be carried by the wind against the shore, with the hope that the bear, when his hind legs should touch bottom, would take himself off; but he was afraid to do so, for it seemed to him that when the brute should be relieved of the necessity of looking after himself, he would turn and look after the boy and girl too closely for their safety.

The very danger, however, that was dreaded more than all others, came when least expected.

Nick had worked the unwieldy craft out in the pond again and had sat down beside Nellie, when, with one of his startling sniffs, the bear made a plunge, which heaved half of his body out of the water and lifted it upon the raft.

As Nick Ribsam had previously remarked, the structure was not built for the accommodation of such passengers, and it began sinking, as the unwonted weight bore it down.

"Don't be scared," said he to his sister; "maybe it's the best thing that could happen; put your hands on my shoulders and keep cool, and we'll swim out yet."

CHAPTER XXXVII.

A BRAVE STRUGGLE.

It was a trying ordeal for little Nellie Ribsam; but she met it with the courage and coolness of her brother. She could not swim a stroke, and, under heaven, everything depended on him. If she should lose her self-control, as would be the case with nine tenths of the girls of her age placed in a similar situation she was likely to drown both herself and her brother.

But so long as she obeyed instructions, and the bear did not interfere, they were safe. She placed her hands on the shoulders of Nick, as he told her to do, and he struck out with his powerful stroke, which he could keep up for an hour if need be.

The difficulty of the situation was deepened tenfold by the anxiety to know what the bear meant to do. He had it in his power to overtake both, and it would have been a trifling matter for him to "dispose" of them in a twinkling: one or two strokes of his immense paw were sufficient.

It was the aim of Nick, therefore, to get away as speedily as possible; and he exerted himself to the utmost, glancing continually over his shoulder, as did the sorely frightened Nellie, who could not avoid a half gasping scream as the waters closed about her to her chin.

But bruin seemed to be absorbed in the management of the raft, which, in fact, was more than he could manage. It was all well enough, so long as it only half supported him; but when he came to lift his huge bulk out of the water the buoyancy of the float was overcome, and it went down.

The bear did not seem to understand it: a moment before he was resting upon a mass of logs, and now, when he looked around, they were invisible, and he was compelled to swim to support himself. He therefore struck out with a loud splash, and had scarcely done so when the light pine logs popped up again like so much cork.

The brute turned around and dropped both paws upon them. Finding they kept afloat, he was too foolish to be content, but repeated his performance, and, as a consequence, speedily found himself pawing the water again to keep his own head above the surface.

This second failure seemed to disgust him, and he paid no further attention to the logs, but headed for the shore, which was so close at hand that he reached it in a minute or two.

This proceeding on the part of the bear, it will be understood, was of great benefit to the brother and sister, who improved it to the utmost. It occupied a brief time, during which Nick swam strongly and steadily, and before the brute was master of the situation Nick's feet touched bottom, and, taking the hand of Nellie in his own, they walked ashore.

"Where is he?" asked the girl, the moment their feet rested on dry land.

"He isn't far off," replied Nick, "and I don't think he cares to disturb us, but I would rather keep him at a distance."

It may be set down as certain that Nick and Nellie were never in such serious peril from the beast as they believed. The bear was of the ordinary black kind, found in the Middle States, which is not particularly savage, and often passes a person without offering him harm.

It is only when the hunter and his dogs assail the brute, or when he is driven by hunger, that he will boldly attack a person.

Besides this, the animal of which I am speaking, had, no doubt, been routed out of his lair in the woods by the approach of the fire, and it was the most he could do to reach the pond in time to save himself. This accounted for his excessive fatigue, which made him loth to enter the water, where he knew he must swim, and which caused him, after entering it, immediately to make for the raft, that he might avail himself of its support.

He had no purpose of molesting the children, and was too indolent to resent the insignificant attack made upon him by Nick with the stick.

But it was not to be supposed that the boy and girl could feel any assurance on this point, and their fright was such as would have come to any older person placed as they were.

It was only through the protection of a wonderful Providence that they had escaped thus far from the fate of hundreds who, in different parts of the country, fell victims to the innumerable forest fires.

When the two emerged from the water, they saw nothing of the bear that had caused them so much disquietude. He had probably headed for the other side of the pond, and was now shut out from view by the volume of smoke which intervened.

"He'll be here after us," said the alarmed Nellie, whose nervousness was excusable; "and I wish you would hurry away."

"I don't think there is any need to be scared, after all," replied her brother; "the bear has all he can do to look after himself, without bothering us."

The fugitives were in a pitiable plight. Nellie's garments were soaked by the water through which she had passed, but the heavy heat of the air prevented her suffering from cold, though the clinging garments caused her to feel ill at ease; and, like her tidy mother, she longed to be at home, that she might change them for clean, dry ones.

When Nick found they had to leave the raft, he caught up his shoes, with the stockings stuffed in them, and, hastily tying the strings together, slung them around his neck. He did not forget, in the excitement of the moment, that they were indispensable.

But there was no way of saving coat, vest and hat, without running more risk than any one ought to run, and the lad let them go, hoping that, possibly, he might recover them after a time.

He had scarcely set his feet upon the ground, when he took them off again. The earth was baking hot to the water's edge, and a live ember, which the ashes concealed from sight, was revealed when the bare foot was placed upon it.

Nick cooled his blistering toes, and then, as quick as possible, drew on his wet shoes and stockings.

"I would be in a pretty fix if barefoot," said he, "I wouldn't have been able to walk home through these woods for a week or less."

It was plain to be seen that the fury of the conflagration had spent itself, so far as it affected this portion of the wood. That tornado of the flame, which swept everything before it, had leaped across the pond, and was speeding onward until it should die out from want of fuel.

In its path was the blackness of desolation. The trees were still burning, but it was in a smoldering, smoking way, with blazing branches here and there, dropping piecemeal to the ground. The flames, which charged forward as they do through the dry prairie grass, had passed by, and the brother and sister had now the opportunity to attempt to reach home.

But it would be hard to overestimate the distress caused by the atmosphere which the forest fires left behind them. There are many gases and vapors which we cannot breathe; but the trouble about smoke is that although we can manage to get along with it when it is not too dense, it is excessively irritating to the lungs.

Several minutes passed, during which little trouble was experienced, and then the two were forced to cough and gasp until they almost sank to the ground from exhaustion. Occasionally the vapor would lift, and, floating away, leave the air below comparatively pure, and then the black and blue atmosphere, heavy with impurities, would descend and wrap them about as with a garment.

"There's one thing sure," said Nick, when he found himself able to speak with some degree of comfort.

"What is that?" asked his sister.

"This will gradually get better and better."

"I don't see how it can get any worse," was the truthful answer of Nellie, who felt as though she had stood all she could bear.

Since the danger of being caught in the flames was gone, the two were at liberty to venture in any direction they chose.

"We'll make the start, any way!" said Nick, with his old resolution of manner; "keep close to me, and, if you see any new bears, don't run into the woods to hide without saying something to me."

CHAPTER XXXVIII.

BEAR AND FORBEAR.

"See here," said Nick Ribsam, stopping suddenly, after taking only a few steps, "I don't like this idea of going home and leaving so many of my clothes behind. That's a good coat and vest, and the hat is my Sunday one."

"You ain't going back to get them, Nick, when the bear is waiting for you!" exclaimed the sister; "if you do, I just think you haven't got any sense at all—now there! that's all there is about *that*."

This was a severe denunciation, but it did not deter the lad from turning directly about and hurrying to the spot where he had landed, when forced to help Nellie ashore.

A strong breeze was still blowing, so that the craft, whether the bear was clinging to it or not, would be sure to come to land again. Nick did not know that the animal had left it, and he was not foolish enough to invite the beast to assail him.

The logs, relieved from their burden, were floating over the surface, and the lad caught sight of them but a short distance off, steadily approaching the shore.

"The raft must have gone under with the coat, vest, and hat," he said, watching the floating mass, "and I should think my clothes would have been lost; but there is something on the logs that looks like my coat and vest. It would be odd if they had kept their place."

Naturally, the whole attention of Nick was absorbed in this matter; and, when he found that the wind was carrying the raft and its freight toward another point, he moved along the margin so as to anticipate its arrival.

As he did so, like the renowned Captain John Smith when pursued by Powhatan's warriors, he paid no attention to where his feet led him. He was studying the raft, as best he could through the smoky darkness, and, knowing the shore as well as he did, he saw no need of looking downward.

All at once his feet struck a large, soft mass, and, before he could check himself, he pitched headlong over it, as though it were a bale of cloth in his path. The nimble boy was on his feet like a flash, and, quick as he was, he was not a moment too soon.

He had caught the ominous growl, and he knew the bear had got in his way again, as it had persisted in doing before.

It did seem singular that the boy and bruin should meet so often, and it may be that the animal, that was resting himself, lost patience over such persecution, for he raised his huge body and made for the frightened boy.

It was an alarming situation for the latter, who did not lose his presence of mind. He knew much of the nature of the animal, though he had never before been brought face to face in this fashion with a wild one.

Desperate as was the haste with which Nick Ribsam fled, he did not forget to run directly away from his sister, so as to prevent her becoming involved in this new danger.

Nor did the lad make any outcry, that could only have resulted in frightening her, but he simply devoted all his energy to getting away from his pursuer, whose whole savage nature seemed to have been aroused by the last disturbance.

Who shall not say that bruin did not identify the youngster as the one that had rapped him so smartly over the snout when he was seeking a resting-place on the raft? If such were the fact, it cannot be wondered that the beast pursued the fellow with such persistency.

127

Nick Ribsam was considered a rapid runner by his playmates, but it took only a minute or two for him to find out he was no match for his pursuer, who, starting only a short distance to the rear, was overhauling him "hand-over-hand."

The boy hoped that the scorching earth would keep the beast from chasing him with too much ardor, but it did not; and, as there was no other recourse, he ran to a sapling, up which he climbed with the celerity of a monkey.

Even as it was, it was within a second of being too late. The bear was so close that, rising on his haunches, he reached his paws and grasped the lowermost foot of Nick, whose hair fairly rose on end, as he thought for the moment that he was going to be dragged down into the crushing embrace of the dreaded animal.

But, fortunately, the shoe pulled off, and, before the bear could understand it, the supple lad was perched above his reach and looking down upon him.

"Well," said Nick, with a sigh, "this is considerably more than I counted on. I didn't think, from the way you acted in the water, that you were anything but a big coward; but I'm thankful enough you didn't get your claws on me."

The huge creature examined the shoe carefully and, finding there was no boy in it, dropped it to the ground, and, sitting on his haunches, again looked longingly upward at the fellow perched just above his reach, as though he understood what a choice dinner he would afford a bruin of his size.

When he ran out his red tongue and licked his inky snout, Nick could not help laughing.

"Not just yet, old fellow; I'd rather stay here two or three days than come down to you."

When some minutes had passed, Nick began to feel that the situation had nothing funny in it at all. What more likely than that the beast, having made up his mind to take the next meal off a plump boy, would stay there until that same boy would be unable to keep his perch any longer, and would drop of his own accord, like a ripe apple.

The question was a serious one indeed, and while the lad was trying hard to determine what was best to do, he heard Nellie calling to him. She, too, was becoming impatient over the long separation and was coming to find out what it meant.

Nick shouted back for her not to approach, explaining that he was up a tree with a bear watching him, and that if she came any nearer the animal would be sure to change his attention to her.

This was enough to keep any one at a respectful distance, but, when Nellie Ribsam heard the alarming announcement, she was determined on one thing: she would see for herself what sort of a picture was made by a boy up a tree with a black bear watching him as the one watched her two years before.

Nick having warned her against coming any nigher, it followed that the temptation to do so was irresistible.

The lifting of the smoke had let in some sunlight, and it did not take her long to reach a position from which she could look on the interesting scene.

"Nick! Nick!" she called, in a guarded voice, not intended for the ears of the bear.

The boy, alarmed for his sister's safety, turned toward the quarter whence it came, and saw the white face peering from behind the trunk of a tree no more than a hundred feet distant. He instantly gesticulated for her to keep out of sight.

"You have done a silly thing, Nellie," said he, impatiently; "the bear is sure to see you, and if he does, it will be the last of you."

"But I don't mean he shall see me," said the brave but not very prudent girl; "if he looks around, why I'll dodge my head back—My gracious! he's looking now!"

And Nellie threw her head so far from the side around which she was peeping, that, if the bear had looked sharp, he would have detected the somewhat bedraggled hat on the other side of the charred trunk.

Nick called to her to be more careful, as he plainly discerned her hat, and the head-gear vanished.

The lad's fear was now on account of his sister, for he knew that so long as he himself could maintain his position in the tree, so long was he safe. The bear species cannot climb trees whose trunks are so small that their claws meet around them, and although this brute scratched at the sapling as though he meditated an attempt, yet he made none, but sat still, looking wistfully upward, and probably hopeful that the boy perched there would soon come down.

"Keep yourself out of sight!" called Nick to Nellie, "for you can't do anything to help me."

The girl understood this, and she began to believe, with Nick, that she had done an exceedingly foolish thing in venturing into the bear's field of vision in this fashion.

And what was to be the end of this singular and most uncomfortable condition of affairs?

CHAPTER XXXIX.

CONCLUSION.

For a half hour the situation remained unchanged. Nick Ribsam kept his perch in the branches of the sapling, and, before the end of the time named, he found the seat becoming so uncomfortable that he was sure he could not bear it much longer.

The narrow limb on which he rested, while he held himself in place by grasping the sapling itself, seemed to grow narrower and sharper, while his own weight increased, until he believed it would be preferable to let go and hang on with his hands.

It was not much better with Nellie, who had awakened to such a sense of her position that she did not dare to do more than peep out from where she stood, at rare intervals, quickly drawing back her head lest the savage animal should see her.

The bear himself showed a patience which was astonishing, and was like that of the Esquimau, who never stirs a muscle for hour after hour, while sitting beside the air-hole in the ice, waiting for the seal to show his nose above the surface.

Bruin moved more slightly now and then, but went no more than a dozen yards from the tree, and seemed never to take his eyes from his victim for more than a second or two.

During these trying minutes, the smoke sometimes filled the air scarcely less than before and the eyes of the brother and sister smarted and stung and shed tears, and their lungs became sore from continual coughing, rendered the more distressing in the case of Nellie, who was obliged to suppress the noise by cramming her handkerchief in her mouth.

But during the same period, the wits of Nick Ribsam were not idle. He had thought of sending Nellie home to bring her father to his assistance, but he was restrained by the fear that the bear would detect her, and, even if she should get away, he doubted whether she would be able to find her way through the woods to the open country beyond.

Here and there the trees were burning, and the dry limbs lay on the ground, giving out the red glow of smoldering embers, or sending out little twists of smoke to join the enormous mass of vapor which hung like a pall over so many square miles of country.

Nellie, for the twentieth time, leaned her head forward and looked out from behind the tree trunk that sheltered her. She saw the bear sitting on his haunches some twenty feet away, looking steadily upward, as though he were a charred stump, which could never change its posture or position. Nick rested uneasily on the narrow limb, when he made a movement which the quick-witted girl knew at once meant that he had resolved on trying to do something for himself.

Carefully freeing his legs from the branch, he lowered himself so that he hung by his hands, within ten feet of the ground. Hanging only a second or two, he let go and dropped lightly upon his feet.

The whole thing took less than a minute, but the bear had observed it almost as quickly as did Nellie, and the minute the lad struck the ground the beast was lumbering toward him.

Poor, terrified Nellie screamed and ran from behind the tree, certain that it was all over with her brave brother; but the latter did not despair by any means. With astonishing celerity, he dashed to where a large pine branch lay on the ground, burned in two; and catching up one of the pieces, which was so hot that it scorched his fingers, he whirled it about with such quickness that the glowing end made one steady, even wheel of fire about his head. He recalled his experience in the woods two years before when hunting the other bear.

While doing this, bruin was advancing rapidly on the boy, who kept circling the torch until the beast was within ten feet, by which time the stick was blazing as though it were a pine knot.

Then, with a boyish shout, Nick extended his arm at full length, pointing the flaming torch straight at the head of his foe, as though he held a Damascus sword of needle-like sharpness which he meant to drive through the iron skull, and he strode directly at the beast with the step of a conqueror.

Every animal, wild or domestic, dreads fire, and this strange attack was more than the bear could stand. Without the least attention to dignity, he turned about and swung off toward the lake, doubtless of the opinion that there alone he could find safety from the element that drove him thither in the first place.

Nick shouted and broke into a run, and the bear did the same! Just under the tree, the lad stopped and put on his shoe, which had been somewhat damaged by the claws of the brute. Then, being well shod and in no further danger from the animal, on which he had turned the tables so unexpectedly, Nick joined his sister, still carrying his torch as a precaution in the event of bruin's changing his mind and making after him.

But there was no danger of anything of the kind, and the bear was not seen to look behind him, even to learn whether the pursuit was kept up.

"I guess I will give over my hunt for the rest of my clothes till some better time," said Nick, once more taking the hand of Nellie and starting up the bank of the stream which fed the pond, toward the bridge that had burned some time before.

By carefully picking their path they reached it without mishap, being on the southern side, so that it was not necessary to ford it in order to continue the road homeward.

The structure was an ordinary one, consisting of a single uncovered span, so that its loss was not serious, except on account of the inconvenience it would cause.

The two stood several minutes looking upon the ruins, that were not very extensive, but their chief interest centered around the carcass of the mare lying at the bottom of the creek, where it had floated against the shore.

The children were naturally attached to the animal, and there were tears in their eyes, when, with a deep sigh, they turned away and climbed up the steep bank to the level of the road and started for home.

They had reason to doubt their ability to force their way through the several miles of forest remaining between them and the open country beyond, but they were resolved to do their utmost, for they dreaded staying any longer in the section where they had suffered and escaped so much.

As has been stated, the fury of the conflagration had expended itself, and there was nothing to be feared from the scorching flames, which had confronted and endangered them shortly after they entered the woods, on their return.

The road was strewn with burning debris, and many a time they were forced to stop, in doubt whether they could get by the obstruction but some way always opened: they would find a point where it could be leaped, or they would flank it by a little circuit through the woods themselves.

In this manner they toiled on until half the distance was passed, when they were brought to a stand-still by a discovery which took away their breath for the time.

They saw the ruins of something which they did not recognize until they drew near, when they discovered that an ordinary farmer's wagon, with its two horses, had been burned. Little more than the iron work of the body was left, and the animals seemed to have gone down side by side, where they lay burned and burst open by the flames, that were less merciful to them than to the brother and sister who had made such a gallant fight for life.

The sight was sad enough, but it was rendered tenfold more so by the figure of the driver, only a few rods distant. When his team gave out he had probably leaped to the ground and started to run from the fire, but was overtaken and perished miserably.

"How thankful we ought to be!" said Nellie, in a subdued voice, as they moved forward again.

"So I am," was the fervent response of Nick, whose heart was melted with pity for the unfortunate stranger, and with thankfulness that he and Nellie had been selected by Heaven for such a signal display of mercy.

They were in constant dread of coming upon similar scenes, but they were spared the sight, and, at the end of about an hour from the time of leaving the bridge, they emerged into the open country, where they were near their own home.

The afternoon was pretty well gone, and the sky still wore that impressive appearance which we all remember well; but it was not so marked as a short time before, and was rapidly passing away.

There was a great deal of smoke drifting and floating through the air, but it caused less inconvenience and annoyance than it did when they fled to the pond for safety.

The children gave another expression of their gratitude, and then hastened toward the humble home, which was, indeed, the dearest spot on earth to them.

The parents were full of anxiety, though they hoped that Nick had seen the danger, and had stayed in Dunbarton with horse and carriage.

But the couple stood at the gate, shading their eyes, and looking yearningly down the road, in the hope of catching sight of the loved forms of the brave children.

When they saw and recognized the figures, they rushed forth to meet them, with swelling hearts. Father and mother pressed them to their breasts, and the eyes of all were streaming with tears, for of Nick and Nellie might it not be said—"For these, my children, were dead, and are alive again: they were lost, and they are found?"

When Nick had told the whole wonderful story, the father took his hand and said in his native tongue:

"My boy, I have taught you that God helps them that help themselves. I am glad that at no time, so far as I can gather, did you despair. You and Nellie have been tried by fire, and have come out as pure gold. Heaven be praised for its mercies. The lesson you have learned will go with you through life. Never despair, but press onward and upward, and the reward shall be yours at last."

And what did the good man say but that which our own beloved and mourned poet has so beautifully limned in lines that shall be as immortal as his own fragrant deeds and revered memory?

> Footprints, that perhaps another,
> Sailing o'er life's solemn main,
> A forlorn and shipwrecked brother,
> Seeing, shall take heart again.
> Let us then be up and doing,
> With a heart for any fate,
> Still achieving, still pursuing,
> Learn to labor and to wait.

THE END.

The second volume of the Wild-Woods Series will be "On the Trail of the Moose."

THE FAMOUS CASTLEMON BOOKS.

BY

HARRY CASTLEMON.

No author of the present day has become a greater favorite with boys than "Harry Castlemon:" every book by him is sure to meet with hearty reception by young readers generally. His naturalness and vivacity lead his readers from page to page with breathless interest, and when one volume is finished the fascinated reader, like Oliver Twist, asks "for more."

*** Any volume sold separately.

GUNBOAT SERIES. By Harry Castlemon. 6 vols., 12mo. Fully illustrated. Cloth, extra, printed in colors. In box **$7 50**

Frank, the Young Naturalist	**1 25**
Frank in the Woods	**1 25**
Frank on the Prairie	**1 25**
Frank on a Gunboat	**1 25**
Frank before Vicksburg	**1 25**
Frank on the Lower Mississippi 1 25	

GO AHEAD SERIES. By Harry Castlemon. 3 vols., 12mo. Fully illustrated. Cloth, extra, printed in colors. In box **$3 75**

Go Ahead; or, The Fisher Boy's Motto **1 25**
No Moss; or, The Career of a Rolling Stone **1 25**
Tom Newcombe; or, The Boy of Bad Habits **1 25**

ROCKY MOUNTAIN SERIES. By Harry
Castlemon. 3 vols., 12mo. Fully illustrated. Cloth,
extra, printed in colors. In box **$3 75**

Frank at Don Carlos' Rancho 1 25
Frank among the Rancheros 1 25
Frank in the Mountains   1 25

SPORTSMAN'S CLUB SERIES. By Harry
Castlemon. 3 vols., 12mo. Fully illustrated. Cloth,
extra, printed in colors. In box **$3 75**

The Sportsman's Club in the Saddle   1 25
The Sportsman's Club Afloat   1 25
The Sportsman's Club among the Trappers 1 25

FRANK NELSON SERIES. By Harry Castlemon
3 vols. 12mo. Fully illustrated. Cloth, extra, printed
in colors. In box **$3 75**

Snowed Up; or, The Sportsman's Club in the Mts.   **1 25**
Frank Nelson in the Forecastle; or, The Sportsman's
Club among the Whalers   **1 25**
The Boy Traders; or, The Sportsman's Club among
the Boers   **1 25**

BOY TRAPPER SERIES. By Harry Castlemon.
3 vols., 12mo. Fully illustrated. Cloth, extra, printed
in colors. In box **$3 75**

The Buried Treasure; or, Old Jordan's "Haunt"   **1 25**
The Boy Trapper; or, How Dave Filled the Order **1 25**
The Mail Carrier   **1 25**

ROUGHING IT SERIES. By Harry Castlemon.
3 vols., 12mo. Fully illustrated. Cloth, extra, printed
in colors. In box **$3 75**

George in Camp; or, Life on the Plains   **1 25**

George at the Wheel; or, Life in a Pilot House.   **1 25**
George at the Fort; or, Life Among the Soldiers. **1 25**

ROD AND GUN SERIES. By Harry Castlemon.
3 vols., 12mo. Fully illustrated. Cloth, extra, printed
in colors. In box **$3 75**

     Don Gordon's Shooting Box 1 25
     Rod and Gun   **1 25**
     The Young Wild Fowlers   **1 25**

FOREST AND STREAM SERIES. By Harry
Castlemon. 3 vols., 12mo. Fully illustrated. Cloth,
extra, printed in colors. In box **$3 75**

     Joe Wayring at Home; or, Story of a Fly Rod   **1 25**
     Snagged and Sunk; or, The Adventures of a Canvas
     Canoe   **1 25**
     Steel Horse; or, The Rambles of a Bicycle   **1 25**

WAR SERIES. By Harry Castlemon. 3 vols.,
12mo. Fully illustrated. Cloth, extra, printed in
colors. In box **$3 75**

     True to his Colors   **1 25**
     Rodney, the Partisan 1 25

OUR FELLOWS; or, Skirmishes with the Swamp
Dragoons. By Harry Castlemon. 16mo. Fully illustrated
Cloth, extra, printed in colors. In box **1 25**

     Marcy, the Blockade Runner 1 25

ALGER'S

RENOWNED BOOKS.

BY

HORATIO

ALGER, Jr.

Horatio Alger, Jr., has attained distinction as one of the most popular writers of books for boys, and the following list comprises all of his best books.

*** Any volume sold separately.

RAGGED DICK SERIES. By Horatio Alger, Jr. 6 vols., 12mo. Fully illustrated. Cloth, extra, printed in colors. In box **$7 50**

Ragged Dick; or, Street Life in New York	**1 25**
Fame and Fortune; or, The Progress of Richard Hunter	
Mark, the Match Boy; or, Richard Hunter's Ward	**1 25**
Rough and Ready; or, Life among the New York Newsboys	**1 25**
Ben, the Luggage Boy; or, Among the Wharves	**1 25**
Rufus and Rose; or the Fortunes of Rough and Ready	**1 25**

TATTERED TOM SERIES. (First Series.) By Horatio Alger, Jr. 4 vols., 12mo. Fully illustrated Cloth, extra, printed in colors. In box **5 00**

Tattered Tom; or, The Story of a Street Arab	**1 25**
Paul, the Peddler; or, The Adventures of a Young Street Merchant	**1 25**
Phil, the Fiddler; or, The Young Street Musician	**1 25**
Slow and Sure; or, From the Sidewalk to the Shop	**1 25**

TATTERED TOM SERIES. (Second Series.) 4 vols., 12mo. Fully illustrated. Cloth, extra, printed in colors. In box **$5 00**

Julius; or the Street Boy Out West	**1 25**
The Young Outlaw; or, Adrift in the World	**1 25**
Sam's Chance and How He Improved It	**1 25**
The Telegraph Boy	**1 25**

LUCK AND PLUCK SERIES. (FIRST SERIES.)
By Horatio Alger, Jr. 4 vols., 12mo. Fully illustrated
Cloth, extra, printed in colors. In box **$5 00**

> **Luck and Pluck;** or John Oakley's Inheritance   1 25
> **Sink or Swim;** or, Harry Raymond's Resolve   1 25
> **Strong and Steady;** or, Paddle Your Own Canoe.   1 25
> **Strive and Succeed;** or, The Progress of Walter Conrad 1 25

LUCK AND PLUCK SERIES. (SECOND
SERIES.) By Horatio Alger, Jr. 3 vols., 12mo.
Fully illustrated. Cloth, extra, printed in colors. In
box **$5 00**

> **Try and Trust;** or, The Story of a Bound Boy   1 25
> **Bound to Rise;** or Harry Walton's Motto   1 25
> **Risen from the Ranks;** or, Harry Walton's Success 1 25
> **Herbert Carter's Legacy;** or, The Inventor's Son. 1 25

CAMPAIGN SERIES. By Horatio Alger, Jr. 3
vols., 12mo. Fully illustrated. Cloth, extra, printed
in colors. In box **$3 75**

> **Frank's Campaign;** or, The Farm and the Camp 1 25
> **Paul Prescott's Charge**   1 25
> **Charlie Codman's Cruise**   1 25

BRAVE AND BOLD SERIES. By Horatio
Alger, Jr. 4 vols., 12mo. Fully illustrated. Cloth,
extra, printed in colors. In box **$5 00**

> **Brave and Bold;** or, The Story of a Factory Boy   1 25
> **Jack's Ward;** or, The Boy Guardian   1 25
> **Shifting for Himself;** or, Gilbert Greyson's Fortunes 1 25
> **Wait and Hope;** or, Ben Bradford's Motto   1 25

PACIFIC SERIES. By Horatio Alger, Jr. 4
vols. 12mo. Fully illustrated. Cloth, extra, printed
in colors. In box **$5 00**

> **The Young Adventurer;** or, Tom's Trip Across the Plains 1 25
> **The Young Miner;** or, Tom Nelson in California   1 25
> **The Young Explorer;** or, Among the Sierras   1 25

Ben's Nugget; or, A Boy's Search for Fortune. A
Story of the Pacific Coast   **1 25**

ATLANTIC SERIES. By Horatio Alger, Jr. 4
vols., 12mo. Fully illustrated. Cloth, extra, printed
in colors. In box **$5 00**

The Young Circus Rider; or, The Mystery of Robert Rudd **1 25**
Do and Dare; or, A Brave Boy's Fight for Fortune   **1 25**
Hector's Inheritance; or, Boys of Smith Institute   **1 25**
Helping Himself; or, Grant Thornton's Ambition   **1 25**

WAY TO SUCCESS SERIES. By Horatio
Alger, Jr. 4 vols., 12mo. Fully illustrated. Cloth,
extra, printed in colors. In box **$5 00**

Bob Burton   **1 25**
The Store Boy   **1 25**
Luke Walton   **1 25**
Struggling Upward 1 25

Five Hundred Dollars Legacy. By Horatio
Alger, Jr. 12mo. Fully illustrated. Cloth, extra,
printed in colors **1 25**

**A
New Series
of Books.**

**Indian Life
and
Character
Founded on
Historical
Facts.**

By Edward T. Ellis.

*** Any volume sold separately.

BOY PIONEER SERIES. By Edward S. Ellis.
3 vols., 12mo. Fully illustrated. Cloth, extra, printed
in colors. In box **$3 75**

Ned in the Block House; or, Life on the Frontier   **1 25**
Ned in the Woods. A Tale of the Early Days in the West **1 25**
Ned on the River   **1 25**

DEERFOOT SERIES. By Edward S. Ellis. In
box containing the following. 3 vols., 12mo. Illustrated **$3 75**

Hunters of the Ozark   **1 25**
Camp in the Mountains 1 25
The Last War Trail   **1 25**

LOG CABIN SERIES. By Edward S. Ellis.
3 vols., 12mo. Fully illustrated. Cloth, extra, printed
in colors. In box **$3 75**

Lost Trail   **$1 25**
Camp-Fire and Wigwam 1 25
Footprints in the Forest   **1 25**

WYOMING SERIES. By Edward S. Ellis. 3
vols., 12mo. Fully illustrated. Cloth, extra, printed
in colors. In box **$3 75**

Wyoming   **1 25**
Storm Mountain   **1 25**
Cabin in the Clearing   **1 25**
Through Forest and Fire. By Edward S. Ellis.
12mo. Fully illustrated. Cloth, extra, printed in colors **1 25**

By C.A. Stephens.

Rare books for boys—bright, breezy, wholesome and instructive; full of adventure and incident, and information upon natural history. They blend instruction with amusement—contain much useful and valuable information upon the habits of animals, and plenty of adventure, fun and jollity.

CAMPING OUT SERIES. By C.A. Stephens.
6 vols., 12mo. Fully illustrated. Cloth, extra, printed in colors. In box **$7 50**

Camping Out. As recorded by "Kit"	1 25
Left on Labrador; or The Cruise of the Schooner Yacht "Curfew." As recorded by "Wash"	1 25
Off to the Geysers; or, The Young Yachters in Iceland As recorded by "Wade"	1 25
Lynx Hunting. From Notes by the author of "Camping Out"	1 25
Fox Hunting. As recorded by "Raed"	1 25
On the Amazon; or, The Cruise of the "Rambler." As recorded by "Wash"	1 25

By J.T. Trowbridge.

These stories will rank among the best of Mr. Trowbridge's books for the y**** and he has written some of the best of our juvenile literature.

JACK HAZARD SERIES. By J.T. Trowbridge. 6 vols., 12mo. Fully Illustrated. Cloth, extra, printed in colors. In box	**$7 50**
Jack Hazard and His Fortunes	1 25
A Chance for Himself; or, Jack Hazard and his Treasure	1 25
Doing His Best	1 25
Fast Friends	1 25
The Young Surveyor; or, Jack on the Prairies	1 25
Lawrence's Adventures Among the Ice Cutters Glass Makers, Coal Miners, Iron Men and Ship Builders	1 25

Suitable for Girls between the Ages of 12 and 15.

Ways and Means. A Story for girls. By Margaret
Vandegrift. With four illustrations. 12mo.
Cloth, extra **1 50**

The Queen's Body-Guard. A Story for Girls. By
Margaret Vandegrift. With four illustrations. 12mo.
Cloth, extra **1 50**

Rose Raymond's Wards. A Story for Girls. By
Margaret Vandegrift. Illustrated with four engravings
on wood. 12mo. Cloth, extra **1 50**

Doris and Theodora. A Story for Girls. By Margaret
Vandegrift. Illustrated with four engravings on
wood. 12mo. Cloth, extra **1 50**

Dr. Gilbert's Daughters. A Story for Girls. By
Margaret Harriet Mathews. Illustrated with four engravings
on wood. 12mo. Cloth, extra **1 50**

Esther's Fortune. A Romance for Girls. By Lucy
C. Lillie. Illustrated. 12mo. Cloth, extra, brown
and gold **1 50**

Helen Glenn; or, My Mother's Enemy. A Story for
Girls. By Lucy C. Lillie. Illustrated with eight illustrations
12mo. Cloth, extra **1 50**

The Squire's Daughter. By Lucy C. Lillie. 12mo.
Illustrated. Cloth, extra **1 50**

For Honor's Sake. By Lucy C. Lillie. 12mo.
Illustrated. Cloth, extra **1 50**

Marion Berkley. A Story for Girls. By Lizzie B.
Comins (Laura Caxton). 12mo. Illustrated. Cloth,
extra, brown and gold **1 25**

Hartwell Farm. A Story for Girls. By Lizzie B. Comins (Laura Caxton). 12mo. Illustrated. Cloth, extra, brown and gold **1 25**

THE HANDSOMEST AND CHEAPEST GIFT BOOKS.

The "Bells" Series.

The "BELLS" Series has been undertaken by the publishers with a view to issue original illustrated poems of a high character, at a price within the reach of all classes.

    Small 4to. Cloth, gilt edges $1 50
    Ivory surface   1 50
    Embossed calf, gilt edges   1 50

GEMS FROM TENNYSON.

By ALFRED TENNYSON. Elegantly illustrated by Hammatt Billings.

BEAUTIES OF TENNYSON.

By ALFRED TENNYSON. Elegantly illustrated with twenty engravings, from original drawings by Frederic B. Schell. Beautifully printed on the finest plate paper.

FROM GREENLAND'S ICY MOUNTAINS.

By BISHOP HEBER. Elegantly illustrated with twenty-two engravings, from original drawings by Frederic B. Schell. Beautifully printed on the finest plate paper.

LADY CLARE.

By ALFRED TENNYSON. Elegantly illustrated with twenty-two engravings, from original drawings by Alfred Fredericks, F.S. Church, Harry Fenn, F.B. Schell, E.P. Garret and Granville Perkins. Beautifully printed on the finest plate paper.

THE NIGHT BEFORE CHRISTMAS.

By CLEMENT C. MOORE. Never before has this popular poem—a favorite with both the old and the young—been presented in such a beautiful dress. It is elegantly illustrated with twenty-two engravings, from original drawings by F.B. Schell, W.T. Smedley, A. Fredericks and H.R. Poore.

BINGEN ON THE RHINE.

By CAROLINE E. NORTON. Elegantly illustrated with twenty-two engravings, from original drawings by W.T. Smedley, F.B. Schell, A. Fredericks, Granville Perkins and E.P. Garrett.

THE BELLS.

By EDGAR ALLAN POE. Elegantly illustrated with twenty-two engravings, from original drawings by F.O.C. Darley, A. Fredericks, Granville Perkins and others.

THE DESERTED VILLAGE.

By OLIVER GOLDSMITH. Elegantly illustrated with thirty-five engravings, from drawings by Hammatt Billings.

THE COTTER'S SATURDAY NIGHT.

By ROBERT BURNS. Elegantly illustrated with fifty engravings, from drawings by Chapman.

Standard Histories.

History of England, from the Accession of James the Second. By Thomas Babington Macaulay. *Standard edition.* With a steel portrait of the author. Printed from new electrotype plates from the last English edition. Being by far the most correct edition in the American market. 5 vols., 12mo. Cloth, extra, per set **$5 00**

Sheep, marbled edges, per set **7 50**

Half Russia (imitation), marbled edges **7 50**

Half calf, gilt **10 00**

History of the Decline and Fall of the Roman Empire. By Edward Gibbon. With notes by Rev. H.H. Milman. *Standard edition.* To which is added a complete Index of the work. A new edition from entirely new stereotype plates. With portrait on steel. 5 vols., 12mo. Cloth, extra, per set **5 00**

Sheep, marbled edges, per set **7 50**

Half Russia (imitation), marbled edges **7 50**

Half calf, gilt, per set **10 00**

History of England, from the Invasion of Julius Cæsar to the Abdication of James the Second, 1688. By David Hume. *Standard edition.* With the author's last corrections and improvements to which is prefixed a short account of his life, written by himself. With a portrait on steel. A

new edition from entirely new stereotype plates. 5
vols., 12mo. Cloth, extra, per set **5 00**

Sheep, marbled edges, per set **7 50**

Half Russia (imitation), marbled edges **7 50**

Half calf, gilt **10 00**

Miscellaneous.

A Dictionary of the Bible. Comprising its Antiquities Biography, Geography, Natural History and Literature. Edited by William Smith, LL.D. Revised and adapted to the present use of Sunday-school Teachers and Bible Students by Revs. F.N. and M.A. Peloubet. With eight Colored maps and 440 engravings on wood. 8vo. Cloth, extra **$2 00**

Sheep, marbled edges **3 00**

Half morocco, gilt top **3 50**

History of the Civil War in America. By the Comte de Paris. Translated with the approval of the author. With maps faithfully engraved from the originals and printed in three colors. 8vo.

Cloth, extra, per vol. **3 50**

Red cloth, extra, Roxburgh style, uncut edges, per vol. **3 50**

Sheep, library style, per vol. **4 50**

Half Turkey morocco, per vol. **6 00**

Volumes I, II, III and IV now ready, put up in a neat box, or any volume sold separately.

The Battle of Gettysburg. By the Comte de Paris. With maps. 8vo. Cloth, extra **1 50**

Comprehensive Biographical Dictionary. Embracing accounts of the most eminent persons of all ages, nations and professions. By E.A. Thomas. Crown 8vo.

Cloth, extra, gilt top **2 50**

Sheep, marbled edges **3 00**

Half morocco, gilt top **3 50**

Half Russia, gilt top **4 50**

The Amateur Photographer. A manual of photographic
manipulations intended especially for beginners
and amateurs, with suggestions as to the choice of
apparatus and of processes. By Ellerslie Wallace,
Jr., M.D. New edition, with two new chapters on
paper negatives and microscopic photography. 12mo.
Limp morocco, sprinkled edges **1 00**

Interest Tables. Containing accurate calculations of
interest at 1/2, 1, 2, 3, 3-1/2, 4, 4-1/2, 5, 6, 7, 8 and 10
per cent. per annum, both simple and compound, on
all sums from $1.00 to $10.00, and from one day to six
years. Also some very valuable tables, calculated by
John E. Coffin. 8vo. Cloth, extra **$1 00**

England, Picturesque and Descriptive. A
Reminiscence of Travel. By Joel Cook, author of
"A Holiday Tour in Europe," "Brief Summer Rambles"
etc. Elegantly illustrated with 487 engravings
on wood. 4to. Cloth, extra **7 50**

Half calf, gilt, marbled edges **10 00**

Half Morocco, full gilt edges **10 00**

Full Turkey morocco, gilt edges **15 00**

The Waverley Novels. By Sir Walter Scott, Bart.
23 vols.

Household Edition. Illustrated. 12mo.

Cloth, extra, per set **23 00**

Half calf, gilt, per set **46 00**

Half morocco, gilt topsp **46 00**

Universe Edition. Printed on thin paper, and containing one illustration to the volume. 25 vols., 12mo.

Cloth, extra, per vol. **75**

World Edition. 12 vols., thick 12mo.

(Sold in sets only.) Cloth, extra **18 00**

Half im't. Russia, marbled edges **24 00**

Captain Jack the Scout; or, The Indian Wars about Old Fort Duquesne. An Historical Novel, with copious notes. By Charles McKnight. With eight engravings. 12mo. Cloth, extra **1 50**

Ladies' and Gentlemen's Etiquette. A Complete Manual of the Manners and Dress of American Society. Containing forms of Letters, Invitations, Acceptances and Regrets. By E.B. Duffey. 12mo.

Cloth, extra **1 50**

The Count of Monte Cristo. By Alexandre Dumas. Complete in one volume, with two illustrations by George G. White. 12mo. Cloth, extra **1 25**

The Iliad of Homer Rendered into English Blank Verse. By Edward, Earl of Derby. With a biographical sketch of Lord Derby by R. Shelton Mackenzie, D.C.L. Popular edition. Two vols. in one. 12mo.

Cloth, extra **$1 50**

Ten Nights in a Bar Room and What I Saw There. By T.S. Arthur. Entirely new edition from new electrotype plates. Illustrated. 12mo.

Cloth, extra **1 25**

Jane Eyre. By Charlotte Brontë (Currer Bell). New Library Edition. With five illustrations by E.M. Wimperis. 12mo. Cloth, extra **1 00**

Shirley. By Charlotte Brontë (Currer Bell). New Library Edition. With five illustrations by E.M. Wimperis. 12mo. Cloth, extra **1 00**

Villette. By Charlotte Brontë (Currer Bell). New Library Edition. With five illustrations by E.M. Wimperis. 12mo. Cloth, extra **1 00**

The Professor, Emma and **Poems.** By Charlotte Brontë (Currer Bell). New Library Edition. With five illustrations by E.M. Wimperis. 12mo.

Cloth, extra, black and gold **1 00**

The four volumes, forming the complete works of Charlotte Brontë, in a neat box.

Cloth, extra, black and gold, per set **4 00**

Fancy cloth, paper label, gilt top, uncut edges **5 00**

Half calf, gilt, per set **8 00**

History of Scotland. (Tales of a Grandfather.) By Sir Walter Scott. 3 vols., 12mo. Cloth, plain **3 00**

Half calf, gilt tops **6 00**

Half morocco, gilt tops **6 00**

Tales of a Grandfather. By Sir Walter Scott, Bart. 4 vols. Uniform with the Waverley Novels.

Household Edition. Illustrated. 12mo.

Cloth, extra, per vol. **1 00**

Sheep, marbled edges, per vol. **1 50**

Half calf, gilt, marbled edges, per vol. **3 00**

Ten Thousand a Year. By Samuel C. Warren, author of "The Diary of a London Physician." A new edition, carefully revised, with three illustrations by George G. White. 12mo. Cloth, extra **$1 50**

The Works of Flavius Josephus. Comprising the Antiquities of the Jews; a History of the Jewish Wars and a Life of Flavius Josephus, written by himself. Translated from the original Greek by William Whiston, A.M. 8vo. Cloth, plain **2 00**

Sheep, marbled edges, library style **3 00**

Embossed leather, "new style" **3 50**

Morocco, gilt edges **5 00**

This is the largest type one volume edition published.

Stanley and the Congo.—Explorations and Achievements in the Wilds of Africa of Henry M. Stanley. Also, a full description of his perilous descent, thrilling adventures and late labors on the Congo River. Together with an account of the expedition to the Central Lake Regions, by Sir Samuel W. Baker, and the journey across Africa in 1874-75, and the discoveries made by Lieut. V.S. Cameron. By J.F. Packard, author of "Young Folks' History of the United States," etc., etc. Fully illustrated. 12mo.

Cloth, extra, black and gold **1 50**

Cookery from Experience. A Practical Guide for

Housekeepers in the Preparation of Every-day Meals, containing more than One Thousand Domestic Recipes, mostly tested by Personal Experience, with Suggestions for Meals, List of Meats and Vegetables in Season, etc. By Mrs. Sara T. Paul. 12mo.

Cloth, extra **1 50**

The Imitation of Christ. By Thomas à Kempis. New and best edition, from entirely new electrotype plates, single column, large, clear type. 18mo.

PLAIN EDITION, ROUND CORNERS.

1. Cloth, extra, red edges **50**
2. French seal, limp, gilt edges **75**
3. Russia, limp, inlaid cross, red and gold edges **2 00**
E. French morocco, padded, gilt edges **1 25**
G. Polished, Persian calf, limp, red and gold edges **1 25**
L. Persian calf, line pattern, limp, red and gold edges **1 50**

The Fireside Encyclopædia of Poetry

COLLECTED AND ARRANGED
By HENRY T. COATES.

27th edition, enlarged and thoroughly revised, and containing portraits of prominent American poets, with facsimiles of their handwriting.

Imperial 8vo., cloth, extra, gilt side and edges **$5 00**
Half calf, gilt   **7 50**
Half morocco, antique, gilt edges   **7 50**
Turkey morocco, antique, full gilt edges **10 00**
Tree calf   **12 00**

Plush, padded sides, nickel lettering   **14 00**

The remarkable success that has attended the publication of "The Fireside Encyclopædia of Poetry"—26 editions having been printed—has induced the author to thoroughly revise it, and to make it in every way worthy of the high place it has attained. About one hundred and fifty new poems have been inserted, and the work now contains nearly fourteen hundred poems, representing four hundred and fifty authors, English and American. The work is now illustrated by finely-engraved portraits of many prominent poets, with their signatures and facsimiles of their handwriting.

The Children's Book of Poetry.

Compiled by HENRY T. COATES.

With nearly 200 illustrations. The most complete collection of poetry for children ever published. 4to.

Cloth, extra, gilt edges **3 00**
Full Turkey morocco, gilt edges **7 50**